RISE

Hinton Thriller Book Three

Lee Dawna

LeeDawna Books, Inc.

First edition

Cover design by Premade Ebook Cover Shop

www.premadeebookcovershop.com

ISBN 978-1-949192-23-0 (paperback)

ISBN 978-1-949192-22-3 (ebook)

Published by LeeDawna Books, Inc.

https://leedawnabooks.com

leedawnabooks@gmail.com

P.O. Box 205, MacArthur WV 25873

RISE

~ This book is dedicated to my editor. Anita, thank you for keeping me off the cliff! ~

Tessa

Death is a strange notion. We all ignore it, doing our best to fight for life, the here and now, the joys we insist are all worth it. None of that pretending stops the inevitable, though. We can put dying out of our minds and pretend our days are important, but death comes for us all in the end. We just don't know when that end will come. Some of us make it to old age and others are gone before they ever have a chance to play at this charade we call life. Then there are those like me, the dead among the living, desolate people who have nothing inside of them but the air their lungs insist upon holding.

I pull my knees tighter into my chest, wrapping my arms around my wet jeans and keeping my eyes trained on the deceiving caress of the river I used to love to wake up beside. Many nights, I'd curl up with Warren and we'd sleep right on this very bank, resting as if we didn't have a care in the world even though we both had many. Now I'm all grown up and my charade is over. There's no place left for me on this earth. No life to pretend at and no love to hold onto. I can't even feel the cool touch of this river anymore. But I don't need to. Long after I'm gone, this water will still be here, flowing from one end of town to the other. It'll wash the pain of loss from Hinton and carry it far away from the memories of the people who call this valley home.

Now that I know where I'm heading and how fast I'm going there, I accept what my fate is. I'm even finding it within myself to be calm. The screams are gone, fading from my lips as dawn peeked over the still burning mountain. I stayed in the park with Gary until the light of this new day cast a sickening pallor over a face that no longer holds a trace of the strength his living body held. He's gone from me. They're all gone. And the only reason I climbed from the depths of this river earlier is because Beth is still alive. If she were dead, I wouldn't have bothered to let the current wash Gary off my skin and clothes, I would have sunk under the surface, watching the fire reflect off the water above me, and never come back up again.

I shiver, not caring to register the shake in my limbs or the threads of pain lacing through my bruised body. After what I saw in the park, every complaint I have is meaningless. Worthless. The brutality of what was done to Gary eclipses everything. It's unfathomable, and it removes all doubt from my mind. Beth is Hinton's killer. No one else would have gotten close enough to kill both Gary and Granger, and no one else would have cause to gut Gary like that. It was Beth, taking out her anger on Gary because of what was done to her dad. She unleashed her fury and strung Gary up, littering the park with his insides in order to repay me for Chopper spreading her dad across the highway. Something I didn't ask Chopper to do and wish he never had. But Beth doesn't care about truth or reason. She never has. She only cares about the reality she tries to convince the rest of us we're living in.

Considering what she's put Hinton through this summer, I'm certain she's proud of herself. I'm as certain of her joy as I am of my guilt. Not a single time since the early days of childhood, when she lied just as easily as she breathed, have I ever called her out for lying. I've never held her accountable for her actions. Instead, I pitied her. Felt sorry for the downturn of her lips even though my own frown was just as deeply etched on my soul. We were born to a bad lot and somehow I focused on her suffering more than my own. Maybe because I had Warren. He was all I ever needed so I didn't much try to make other friends. People were around but it was only Warren who I was close to.

Beth tried to be close to everyone and most didn't want her around. I felt bad for her on account of that. I talked her up whenever anyone would listen and I defended her when they tried to do their own talking, so I'm as guilty of the murders as she is because Beth used the care I had for her to manipulate everyone. It was because of me taking up for her that no one ever challenged her. She'd lie and people would just nod along like they didn't know the words coming out of her mouth were upside down and turned every which way but right. For my part in allowing her to fester like a boil, I'll not allow her to outlive me. The air won't leave my lungs until Beth is dead. She dies, and then I end this charade I'm being forced to live.

I inhale deeply, pulling breath inside my body just to check that I'm still capable of breathing. The light on the far side of the river is now a mix of day and still burning embers dropping down from the sky above me. I watch the red flecks float into the water, their flame going out and the specks of char washing away. Each one carries a part of Warren. Chopper. Men I've loved and ruined, all with the same breaths I'm taking now.

Neither of them deserved to be on that mountain and they wouldn't have been if it weren't for me. I threw my life away when I fell victim to my own insecurities. I dumped Warren, and then I dragged him and the others straight to hell with me. "I'm sorry," I whisper to the ash, digging my fingers into the sides of my legs to keep myself from crawling back into that water to be with him. If there is no afterlife and I'll never see Warren again, I still want to stop breathing. "I'm going to kill Beth, and then I'm coming to find out what lies on the other side."

"There you are," a coarse voice crawls over my cold, wet shoulders. "I knew you'd find your way to the river. You always do."

I loosen the grip I have on my legs. My limbs now free to tremble, my whole body shudders, my ability to breathe losing its way as I slowly spin toward the voice I'd know even if it were muffled under a pillow and buried in a pile of rocks. Heart hamming, I set my eyes on the source. It's hunched against the slope of the bank behind me, form crusted in blood and features hidden by layers of soot. It doesn't matter. I'd know this apparition any which way he came to me. "Warren."

His name falls from my lips and I push up to my feet, moving toward him slowly so as not to spook whatever brought this vision to me. Tears fill the space between us, his and mine. I reach my fingers forward and rest them against his warm skin. "Who were you whispering to?" He wheezes.

"You." I throw my arms around him, crushing my body against his. "I was talking to you. I thought you were gone, Warren. I thought you were with the rest of them and I'd never see you again."

"Me too." He coughs, sliding down the bank, my weight overpowering his ability to stand. He shrugs to the side, toppling onto his back and bringing me down with him.

I keep myself attached to the solidness of this dream and stare into chestnut eyes that I know better than my own. "Warren? Am I dead already, or are you really here?"

His cracked lips do their best to smile. "It's me, baby. I'm here."

My tears wash tracks against his skin, the tight hold of his arms confirming his words are true. "You're alive," I whisper, the torture of thinking he was dead choking its way up my throat. My fists clench. I drag them from around his neck and slam them against his shoulders. "You're alive!" I hit him harder. "I thought you were *dead*. You let me think you died on that mountain!"

His fingers dig into my hips, a gurgling growl rattling up from his chest. "I almost did die, and I'm hurt, so stop hitting me, baby. Just stop, and let me hold you because I thought you died up there too." He pulls me down against him, trapping my fists and holding me close. "I heard you scream, Tess. I heard you scream so many times."

I shove my hands free and tangle my fingers through his matted hair, burying my tear-soaked face in the curve of his neck. "Gary's dead. Gary, Granger, Chopper, they're all dead."

His arms tense, right along with every muscle in his body. "You're sure?"

My voice catches on the lump I can't seem to swallow. "I saw them, Warren. They're all gone and I thought you were too."

His head turns, his nose sliding across the top of my head and his own voice breaking. "I'm sorry, baby. I'm so freaking sorry."

I twist my face up to his. "I don't need you to be sorry, I need you to be alive. I love you, Warren. Every day, for all of my life, I've loved you.

Even when I said I didn't." I press my lips against his. "I thought you died without knowing how sorry I am for hurting you. How sorry I am for ruining the best thing I ever had. I'm so sorry for making you suffer for my sins."

He drags a hand to my face and fists it in my hair, holding me in the heat of his breath. "I'd walk through a thousand fires just to hear you say that." His cracked lips move against mine, the kiss of a resurrected man sweeter than any I've ever had.

He shifts underneath me, his groan one of pain, not pleasure. I try to lift myself away but he holds me in place. "Don't move just yet, baby, I want to feel this. I want to look at you." He runs the tips of his fingers down my cheek. "If it wasn't for hearing you scream and knowing that sound meant you were alive, I wouldn't have made it out of the fire. I hate what you went through but you saved me from burning alive, baby. You brought me to you. Just like you always do."

A sob breaks loose and I lean my forehead onto his. His face is swollen and busted open, his bare torso burned and blood-streaked. "I almost got you killed, Warren. I got all of the others killed and you almost died too."

He grips my chin and pulls my mouth back to his. "I love you too, baby. For all my life. But you couldn't kill me on your best day and this is your worst, so shut up and kiss me because you owe me a heck of a lot of your lips on mine."

~2~

I oblige Warren's demands, the taste of soot on our tongues thick with the salt of our tears. My hands drag up his arms, fingers grazing the raw patch of flesh where the fire left a mark that screams just how close it came to consuming him. His lips pinch and I pull away. "This is your worst day, too. How about we pause a minute and get you cleaned up."

I take off my wet shirt and use it to dab at the whole mess of him. He runs his fingers over my stomach. "This isn't my worst day, Tess. Not by a long shot."

His eyes meet mine and I know which days he thinks are worse. All of the ones when we weren't together. I run my shirt over his face. "How badly are you hurt?"

He coughs, blood splattering onto his lips. "About that bad."

I turn my shirtsleeve inside out and use a clean spot to wipe the blood from his lips. "Let's get up to the road. I'll flag down a car and get you to the hospital, and I'll stay there with you because no one is going to hurt you ever again, Warren. I swear I won't let anyone hurt you."

He tugs on the waist of my jeans. "Come here, baby. I want this time with you because I fought like hell to get here."

I lean over him, doing my best to clean the soot from his mouth and nose. "You're going to keep fighting, Warren, and I'll be right beside you."

He coughs again, blood splattering back across his lips. "Chopper did a number on me. When I came to, there was already smoke everywhere. I was so scared he didn't get you off the mountain, then I heard you scream." His palm cups my cheek. "This is enough for me. Being here with you and seeing you alive is enough. Hearing you admit to loving me makes it all the better." His thumb strokes a gentle caress. "This is all I have left, baby. I can't walk anymore and even if I could, you know I can't go to a hospital. If the club didn't get to me before I got locked up, they'd get me while I was sitting behind bars. I don't want that. I want this. You. Me. And our river."

"No," I cry. "No! You're not leaving me, Warren. Don't you dare die on me!"

~

Bobby Baker is the kind of scum that grows along the edge of a stagnant mudhole. Occasionally an unsuspecting woman walks his way but it never takes more than a step to get his stench kicking up. A few women have tolerated the stink but Bobby never looked once at Beth, let alone twice, so I imagine he missed his chance at ever finding someone to settle down with.

I'm not disappointed that Bobby's truck is the first vehicle I see. He's parked at the base of the mountain, he and several other volunteer firemen digging trenches to help control the blaze. I don't trust the others but Bobby knows when to keep his mouth shut. Especially where I'm concerned. Being a daughter of the Leidolf has its benefits in that way. Or had. But Bobby won't yet know that Gary is dead or that I no longer have a pack of wolves at my back. By the time he realizes anything different, I'll be long gone.

I stay clear of his truck and watch him as he leans on the hood and stares at me. I point at him and then mimic holding a phone up to my ear, pointing at him again and motioning for him to come over to me. His eyes narrow. He pulls his phone from his pocket, holding it up and tilting it back and forth, taunting me. I crook my finger to tell him to come, thrusting it down toward the ground in front of me to let him know I mean for him to come to me right this very second.

He glances up at his brothers on the mountain and then back at me. I point at the ground again and then hold up my hand, counting my fingers down from five. He rolls his eyes and trudges toward me. "I'm sure you've noticed the fire, Tessa, since you look like the one who started what I've spent the whole night fighting." He runs his eyes over my wet clothing stained with soot and Warren's blood. "You look like nothing but trouble and still have the nerve to show up here threatening me?"

I snatch the phone from his hand. "If I had to come over there and pry this out of your fingers, I was going to go ahead and break them in your truck door for making me have to threaten you twice."

He launches a response but I don't care to listen. I walk away, growling at him when he tries to follow. He stops and throws up his hands, letting them fall down to perch on his hips. I keep my distance and watch his every twitch as I dial Chief, glad the lawman has had the same phone number for as long as I can remember. It also helps that I'm good with numbers. "It's Tessa." I keep my voice low so Bobby can't hear. "I need transportation, a doctor, and a safe place to stay. No hospitals. And before you argue that point with me, let me tell you that it was the Northern Charter of the Leidolf who started the fire. I was on the mountain and they ran me off it because they're coming for me, and they're desperate enough to storm straight into your jail and rip me out from behind the bars you're probably thinking about putting around me so wipe away those thoughts and meet me at the second turn-out past the tunnels. On your way, call Dr. Lafferty from Princeton Medical and have her meet us wherever you plan to take me."

Chief grumbles a low response, keeping his voice out of earshot of whoever is causing the commotion wherever he is. I ignore him the same way I ignored Bobby. I don't need to hear what they have to say, I need them to listen to me. Warren's life depends on it.

I hang up on Chief and send him a text. *I'm on Bobby Baker's phone so don't respond. Just call the doctor and then come pick me up.* I send the message and then erase the record of it and the call. I march back to Bobby and hand him the phone. "Thanks."

He takes the device. "Not like I had a choice. But now that you've made your call, you have the time to tell me what part you played in starting this fire."

I meet his stare. "The only part I have in this fire is putting it out, and if you tell anyone you saw me today, you'll be on my list of things to snuff out."

He crosses his arms. "Geez, Tessa. You don't have to keep threatening me. I'm not going to tell anyone I saw you but at some point, I think I deserve to know why I've been out here all night risking my life to keep this town from going up in flames. Where did you even come from?"

I move away from him. "Nowhere. You never saw me."

He grabs my arm. "Wait. Clearly you're in the middle of something so can we meet up once it's over? You know, so you can answer my questions and I can maybe see what I can do for you?"

I glance to the mountainside where we're still out of view of the others. "If I didn't know better, I'd say that while we're out here in the middle of all this, you're still finding time to hit on anything that moves." I level my stare at him and he releases my arm. "It's no secret that I don't like you, Bobby, and you keep reminding me of why. So I do appreciate that you'll be keeping your mouth shut for the greater good of us all. Enough people have died in Hinton already, don't you think?"

He holds up his hand. "I was only asking. And only because I deserve answers after battling this blaze all night."

I shake my head at him. "Too bad I don't have time to waste on you and even if I did, I wouldn't. Warren might meet up with you, though. He doesn't think you're as slimy as I do." I step back toward him. "I'm not saying any of this to you to hurt your feelings. I'm pretty sure you don't have feelings."

A grin spreads over Bobby's face. "I'm pretty sure you're right. Tell Warren I'll be waiting on his story, and he can also throw in a six-pack and a couple bags of chips since I had to battle your mouth on top of dealing with this fire."

I march away from him. If Chief doesn't show up soon, there might not be a Warren left.

~3~

Chief's car pulls onto the shoulder. I emerge from the trees and he scrambles out of the vehicle, raking his glare over me. "Darn it, Tessa. I have eyes watching my every move. Sneaking off to meet you wasn't easy. I thought you said you needed a doctor?"

"I do," I answer. "For Warren."

"Warren?" He looks around. "You call me up out of the blue like I don't already know exactly who started this fire and you expect me to drop everything I'm in the middle of to help *Warren*?" Chief's lips curl as if simply saying the name of the man I love sets his mouth on fire. "Warren and the rest of the snakes you cling to are wreaking havoc in my town and I told you this was exactly what was going to happen! You're a pawn for them to use. Nothing more. Just collateral damage. And make no mistake that Warren sees you in the same light as the rest of them because he's as venomous as they come!"

I stalk toward Chief. "You're the one who needs to make no mistakes here because if you don't get down this bank and help me bring Warren up to your vehicle, I'll make sure you die right next to him."

Chief's jaw grinds. "Is that so?"

I rest my hand atop his service weapon. "It is. Because I have nothing left in this world to lose except for Warren." I slide Chief's gun from the holster, our eyes locked, his questioning and mine as dead as I feel inside. I press the gun into his palm. "I don't want to fight with you and I don't want to hurt you, but I will. I'll do whatever I have to do to save Warren's life."

Chief shoves his gun back in place. "Even if I help you, Warren's still what he is and I'm going to see to it that he's buried under my jail."

I press my finger into his chest. "You're not going to do anything to Warren but save his life, and that's a fact you hang your own life on." I drop my hand and move close enough that my front brushes his. "Those snakes you're so worried about no longer have a head. Gary and Chopper are dead, and my sister is your serial killer."

He blinks, his mouth flopping open. "Beth? Gary..."

I turn away from Chief's gaping maw. "You heard me right, and Warren is this way. We help him first, and then we find my sister. I'm going to gut Beth the same way she gutted Gary."

I duck under the branch of a pine that managed to ward off the embers raining down from the mountain. Chief's footsteps are slow and steady behind me. "Beth?" he asks again, his voice soft. "Honey, how could she kill Gary? Are you sure the club isn't faking all of this to get Chopper out of town and away from the justice he deserves?"

I keep picking my way down the bank. "I watched Freddie blow Chopper's brains out and I was covered in Gary's guts so yeah, I'm sure they're both gone."

Chief grabs hold of my elbow. "Wait a minute. You saw Freddie kill Chopper and Beth kill Gary?"

I yank my elbow free. "If I saw what Beth was doing to Gary, she'd be dead already. And if it weren't for Warren figuring out that Beth is the serial killer, we'd *all* be dead already. So quit stalling. We need to hurry."

Chief shoves a thumb behind his service belt, staying exactly where he is as I trail away from him. "Tessa, you're telling me that *Warren* told you Beth was killing people? And you believe him because why? You think she's strapping one on to rape these women?"

"No," I bite, glaring up at him. "She had a partner with all the equipment she needed, and his head is in a cave on the mountain. Once you see to it that Warren lives, you can go collect Matt Honaker's missing parts."

"Honaker?" Chief blanches. "Beth and Matt? All this puzzling came from *Warren*?"

My nostrils flare. "If you say Warren's name like that one more time I'm going to rip out your tongue. Matt Honaker *is* a rapist because he raped *me*. And your town isn't burning because of the Leidolf. It's exploding because of *Beth*. She started the war and I'm going to finish it, so you wipe that look off your face and you take whatever words are in your mouth and swallow them because Warren is dying down there next to this river and I won't waste time asking you again to help me." I thrust a hand toward the shoreline. "Get your cheating backside down this hill and bring Warren up to your car, or so help me I'll put a bullet in you and me both and let Beth continue to live out her sadistic fantasies with everyone you love."

His feet begin to move. "Darn it, Tessa. I'm here, and I'm going to help you, honey, but I need to call this in and you need to calm down. I'm not your enemy and I never have been. All I ever do is try to help you."

My teeth grind. "I don't need your help. Warren does."

Chief catches up and shoves by me. "Show me where he is so we can get this over with and I can get back to doing my job." He jumps from the bank and onto the rocky shore, holding his hand up to help me down. "You're sure Beth is involved in all of this?"

I let his hand hang limp and jump from the hillside of my own accord, landing on the bank beside him and picking up my pace as I lead him to Warren. The soot-covered man is right where I left him, flat on his back with the tips of his fingers resting in the river. I tried to wet his lips before I left, begging him to drink, but he said it burned too bad, his throat raw from the smoke inhalation. He needs an IV. And I need him to live. "Beth killed all of them, going all the way back to Layla. Let that sink in, Chief. *Beth* is the murderer you've been hunting all these years and she's been babysitting just about every kid in this town. Including yours."

He kneels beside Warren and checks his pulse. "I'm trying real hard not to let that sink in, Tessa. I hope to God that you're wrong."

~

Chief's house is private, set back off the road and tucked into a fifteen-acre wooded tract that borders nothing but more woods. I turn away from the window of the master suite and put my attention back on Warren. He's on Chief's bed, his whole body on full display as Dr. Lafferty applies salve to the burns on his chest and arms. After Chief explained who he was and why he was calling, Dr. Lafferty took directions on how to navigate the old logging roads that lead to the back of this property. She took longer to get here than I liked, but she's here now and Warren is hooked up to an IV I know he needs.

The doctor's eyes meet mine, voice low so as not to wake Warren. She added a sedative to his drip so he'd sleep through the process of his wounds being cleaned. "He'd be better off at a hospital."

As if he heard her, his face pinches into a grimace. My insides clench. I wish he was reacting to the doctor's words, but the only thing Warren is hearing right now is the song of his pain. Chopper beat him down and left him for dead. I move away from my spot by the window and trace my fingers over the outline of his face. He was never fully a boy. Warren has always been a man and he doesn't deserve to be lying in this bed right now. "You're right, Doctor. Warren would get better care at a hospital. Right up to the point when an angry wolf puts a bullet in his skull."

She swallows, putting her skilled hands back to work on the upper part of Warren's left arm where the worst of his burns are. "When Chief Dunbar called me, he said Tessa of the Leidolf told him to." She hazards a glance at me. "You used an alias when you came to let me treat you but I knew who you were. If I hadn't, I wouldn't have come here today."

I narrow my eyes on her. "Warren is Leidolf. If you refuse to help him, I'll bring retribution. For him and the club."

She gets off the bed and removes her gloves. "I didn't say I wasn't going to treat him. I'm here and I'm doing everything I can. What I'm telling you is that I've seen the news coverage of what's happening in this town just like everyone else has. The Leidolf are...something I didn't think they were. But what they are and what they're not doesn't matter. I owe them nothing. I never have. The medical favors I do for them have only ever been out of respect for what I thought they stood for. I don't run to their beck and call because I have to."

I pull the sheet back over Warren's exposed body. I made Chief bring me a bowl of soapy water and I did my best to sponge Warren clean. He was awake for that part and muttered enough inappropriate things that Chief stormed out of his own house. "I'll make sure you're well compensated for putting yourself out, Doctor. But it might be a while before I can get that cash to you, and you're not going to slack off on caring for Warren while you wait for me to grease your palm."

She lifts her hand. "No, that's not what I'm saying. I'm not interested in taking your money. I was just letting you know that I'm here of my own free will because what I want from you is information."

I flip my palms to the ceiling. "Sorry. I'm fresh out."

She takes a tentative step in my direction. "I understand how this works. Trust me when I say I'm happy to stay on the clueless outskirts of the club because I don't want to be dragged into whatever is going on. But you're already in it and up until I saw the footage of the one called Chopper, I didn't think for a single second that a member of the Leidolf had attacked you. But now I'm wondering if my loyalty to them is as displaced as yours. Was it the Leidolf who brutalized you?"

I square my shoulders. Despite what the Northern Charter planned to do to me and so many others, the club I know would never do the kind of harm that was done to me. "The Hinton Charter is innocent, even the one called Chopper, and the man who attacked me is dead."

Her hand jumps to her heart. "Thank God, on all accounts. I didn't want to believe the worst of them but I've been attacked before and by someone I never expected would hurt me." She sits on the bed by Warren's feet and folds her hands in her lap. "The man I married turned violent about a month after the wedding. Looking back, I guess there were signs but nothing ever stood out to me. Then the beatings started, and then he began forcing himself on me." Her fingers tighten around each other. "That's how I met Rick. He stumbled upon me one night after I'd wrapped my car around a telephone pole. He and a few of the others were driving back into Hinton after a run and when they found me, it was clear to them that not all of my bruises were a result of the wreck."

She shifts uncomfortably. "My own husband abused me and I stayed foolishly loyal to him because I was too embarrassed to have to admit that this man I loved was hurting me. Doctors are supposed to be smart. People look up to us. But there I was, a battered woman lying about running from her husband. And not for the first time."

I study the lines of Warren's face. In our relationship, I'm the abuser. "It's a good thing the wolves knew what they were seeing. I'm assuming your husband doesn't beat you anymore?"

She sniffs. "Soon after the wreck, Fritz disappeared. His body was found floating in a pond where he used to go fishing. No one ever questioned his death but I knew from the first moment that he'd been killed. And not just by any of them, I knew it was Rick."

I face her. "If you're asking me for information about who killed your husband, I'm not just clean out, I never had any knowledge of it to begin with."

She blinks, eyes brimming with tears she's attempting not to shed. "The information I want is about Rick's life. I want to know if he's still alive after all the things I've seen on the news because despite telling myself I'd never let myself love anyone again, I love that man." She brushes her hands over her face. "I can't explain it, but we formed a bond the night he helped me from that wreckage. I didn't see Rick again until long after Fritz was dead, but something about the way he looked at me stuck, and I couldn't forget a single thing about him. I went to the Grille looking for him and I found him." Her eyes meet mine, a sad smile etched into her features. "That's how I knew who you were. I've been to the Grille a handful of times to visit Rick, but mostly he comes to me. I never know when he'll show up, I just know that he does. But lately, he hasn't even called me and I'm terrified. Do you know where he is? Or how he is?"

I wish I could help her but even if I knew where Rick was, I couldn't tell her. My club might not love me anymore, but I love them. That's why I wish Warren would have chosen them over me. "I'm dead in the red, Doctor. The only thing I can tell you is that you're not crazy for loving a man like Rick. If you're the praying sort, send up words on his behalf, and maybe spare a few for the rest of us too."

~4~

The brutality of Chopper's attack shows in every plane of Warren's muscled torso. Dr. Lafferty stayed with us last night, keeping him sedated until he woke up this morning pitching a fit. I wanted to fight with him about the IV but the fear in his eyes backed me down. I didn't buck up again until Chief came back. He never said we could make ourselves at home but I did anyway, showering and helping myself to a pair of his wife's sweatpants and a t-shirt. Chief took offense at my attire and I took offense at him having the audacity to think I care about his opinion.

"Well, Chief Dunbar is gone again." Dr. Lafferty leans on the doorframe, a gentle smile resting on her lips. "I'll be leaving soon myself, and I can bring you some clothes back if you want?"

I quietly walk to the bed, pressing a palm to Warren's forehead. He has a fever but it's lower now than it was yesterday. The fluids and rest did him good, his body fighting even when the man himself was unaware because Warren's spirit has always had a will to survive. No matter what came to him, he always made a point of living. "I'm going to find the washing machine and clean the clothes Warren and I came here in. Then Chief can have these clothes back but he's not getting this room back. I'm not moving Warren until he's ready to be moved."

She walks farther into the room. "I agree with your stance on that. This wolf has a long road to healing, though I'm sure he won't walk it any slower than you've walked yours."

I fix my gaze on Warren, every mark on his skin a reminder of what he's endured for me. "He's going to be okay, right?"

She stands beside me. "There's nothing to be done for his ribs and his lungs are most certainly bruised. That's on top of the damage from the smoke inhalation. His throat is going to hurt him for a while and he'll be short of breath. There will be chest pains from the smoke alone, the beating he took only adding to that. Then there are the burns and the twisted ankles." Worry lines crease her forehead. "There could be internal bleeding that I'm not picking up. He needs to be very, very careful." She looks at me. "You understand how serious this is, so make him rest. He doesn't need a rib slicing through a lung. He needs to stay in bed and take the medications I'm leaving. You should take the antibiotics as well. I'm going to assume you no longer have access to what I prescribed for you before?"

I close my fingers around his. "I have access to Warren. That's all I need."

She rests a hand on my shoulder. "I saw the way he looked at you when he brought you to see me that first time. He's as determined to love you as you are to save him, so you're both going to be just fine. I only wish I knew if Rick was too because I keep running through scenarios in my head. On the one hand, I'm sure he has feelings for me even if they aren't as strong as what Warren has for you, which means Rick not calling to reassure me means he *can't* call." She removes her palm. "On the other hand, I'm sure I'm not his one and only and I just might be one of many. None of which he's thinking about in the midst of what the news is reporting the club to be involved in. Neither scenario makes me feel any better." Her lips part into a self-pitying smile. "I'm sure you see women like me all the time in the Grille, hopelessly in love with one club member or the other while said club member just doesn't care at all."

I drag in a breath, offering her what little comfort I can. "I do see infatuated women in the Grille all the time. The single men take them up on what they're offering if they feel like it, but the others don't. That must be why no one's caught Rick with anyone in his arms lately. He's saving himself for his doctor."

She laughs, my words bringing a genuine smile to her face. "Then I guess if I find out Rick hasn't called because he's stuck in a bed like this one, I'll borrow some of your backbone and threaten to kill whoever is housing him."

I shrug. "Everyone will know where I stand from here on out because I'm on a hill that only has one way off it, and how bloody my descent becomes all hinges on whether or not Warren lives or dies."

She picks up one of two oversized tote bags that she came in with, a smile still painted on her lips. "The first time I ever went to Riverside Grille, I asked Rick about you. He said all I needed to know is that if you ever told me to jump, I should attach myself to the ceiling and wait for him to come get me down. I'm starting to understand why he didn't want me to cross paths with you." She winks. "Now that I know what I'm dealing with here, I'll be back tomorrow with more supplies for Warren. When he wakes up, test his tolerance for food. The sooner he's back to eating and drinking, the sooner he'll be ready to come down off that hill with you."

~

With Warren resting and Dr. Lafferty gone, I leave the bedroom and dump my soiled clothes and Warren's filthy pants into the washing machine that's tucked into an oversized closet at the end of the hall. The smoke probably won't wash out of any of our things, but we have nothing else right now and Warren won't be looking for a handout any more than I am. Especially from Chief. With the way the two of them have always hated each other, Warren will strut naked through the middle of town before he wears Chief's clothes.

I add a generous amount of detergent and start the machine, closing the closet doors to keep as much of the noise down as possible. If Warren wakes up, he'll want to get up. He'll want out of this house. There's no place for us to go though. Not while he's in such bad shape.

I make my way to the living room and cross to the bay window that overlooks the backyard. The land is level, something novel in these parts when you start adding the acreage. There's a jungle gym off-center from the basketball court and a large above-ground pool attached to the deck. Despite his affair with Erin, Chief has lived a comfortable life here with his family, providing his boys with the kind of childhood Warren and I never dreamed of because longing for things you'd never have seemed pointless. We just did our best with what we did have, the bulk of that being each other, and we made plans for a future we were certain we'd have together. Funny how not a single thing panned out for us. We became legal adults and life crumbled around us until there wasn't even an us left. I'm to blame for the crumbling and I can never take back my many wrongs. All I can do is set life back to right for Warren.

Tires crunch on the gravel drive and I walk to the window facing the front, sliding a piece of the blind up to check that it's only Chief. He parks by the front porch, face long as he steps out of his vehicle and stares at his house, regret etched deep in the lines of his frown. Not for being a bear to me this morning. He regrets bringing us here.

I meet him at the front door. "I would say something funny, like *hi, honey, glad you're home*, but neither of us would laugh so just come on in and tell me if you found my sister."

He looks over my familiar clothing, tossing his keys into a ceramic tray that looks like one of his kids made it. One of the ones fathered with his wife. "Arnold hasn't seen Beth and neither has anyone else. That either means you're right and she's on the run because she knows you figured it out, or it means you've been getting bad information from someone who has cause to give it to you, and your sister is dead somewhere. Take your pick on which of those makes you feel better."

I push the door shut behind him. "I'm going to pretend you didn't just accuse Warren of being a murderer."

Chief huffs out a breath. "There's no accusing, there's only fact. There are three dead bodies at your house, two in the park, and according to you, several more up on that mountain. I doubt you did any of that killing but there are still powers above me who want to bring you in, and all because everybody knows who you *run* with. The worst of them has a name that starts with W and ends in N. With an A, two Rs, and an E in between."

I tap my chin. "You missed a body. Freddie's is on the tracks by the park. I put several bullets in him to make sure he was good and dead, which is the least of what he deserved for what he did to Chopper. And yeah, that's me excusing Chopper for what he did to the man who pretended to be my father. He was a sperm donor and a poor one at that. Gary is the man deserving of the title of being my dad, and you can find the bodies of the other people I shot out in the train yard."

Chief shoves both of his hands up through his hair, cursing and turning red from the neck up. His teeth grind. "You need to keep your mouth shut, Tessa. I have you in my house. I sent my wife and kids away and you're *in* my house, wearing my wife's clothes. How do you think that's going to look if you're found here? How am I supposed to pretend that I didn't know about anything you're telling me? If you're caught in my house, everyone, including the FBI, is going to think I've been secretive and sneaking off to help you avoid the law because I'm sleeping with you! Why else would I do such foolhardy things as you've got me doing?"

"Keep your voice down," I scold. "With my track record and Warren in your bed, it won't be too hard for you to deny sleeping with me. And with the confession I just gave you, you can settle all the death in this town with one final case. I kill Beth, and then I go away forever while between her and me, you account for every murder in this town. You walk away like a hero and maybe write yourself a book about the two sisters who terrorized your town."

"And just how do you think you're going to go away forever?" he asks. "You think the club you've killed half of is going to let you live in prison? Or do you think you're going to be able to outrun them *and* the law. You might be smart but you're not smart enough to keep yourself one step ahead of all of us."

I don't bother explaining to him that I won't have a need to run anymore. I'll find a way to make Warren live without me and then I'll do the thing I know he'll never forgive me for. I press my palm to Chief's cheek. "Don't worry about me, and don't worry about the words you'll use to describe my sister and me. I don't care what you say about either of us. All I care about is you removing Warren's name from whatever list it needs to come off of because he's not going to jail. You try to take him, for *any* reason, and I'll make you long for the simple days of havoc my sadistic sister has been unleashing this summer."

His jaw grinds. "What did I tell you about threatening me?"

I remove my touch from him and lift my arms out to the side. "Look at me, Chief. I'm a wounded animal in a corner. I have nothing left, so this is all you get. I'll be the harbinger of death one final time and then Hinton can rebuild, with their *virtuous* police chief at the helm. Just remember that you made a promise to me. One you're going to keep. Warren's life and yours are bound together, he lives and so do you. He stays free, and you do too."

$$\sim 5 \sim$$

Chief isn't a perfect man but he's a good one. He cares about Hinton and all the people in it. I've never doubted that. His desire to make the right calls is written in the way the muscle in his jaw ticks when he's fighting the blurring of the lines between what the law says is good and bad and what he knows will be best for Hinton. At one time, he came down on the side of the Leidolf. Not wholly and never unconditionally, but enough that the gray areas were solidly marked.

His jaw loosens, but only a fraction. "I can't fail in this, Tessa. Our town needs answers. Heck, I can't even get the mayor to make a speech to calm anyone down because he's scared to walk out his front door. He has half my men over there patrolling his property while he cozies up inside with his wife."

"Because he's worse than a coward. When this is all over and you come out smelling like the hero, take Mayor's job. Warren will help you. He knows where Mayor's skeletons are hidden."

Chief's teeth clang together. "If I want to be the mayor, I'll get there without owing anything to the likes of that dog you dragged into my bed. See to it that he's gone sooner rather than later because if he isn't, I'll remove him myself." He stomps away, down the hall to one of his boys' rooms. If both of his sons didn't have bunk beds I could have set Warren up there and at least let Chief have his own bed to sleep in, but this is just another twist of the knife of fate. Warren is perched in Chief's house, in the largest and best room. All that matters to me is Warren's life but these two men care about ego and power. Bedrooms aren't just bedrooms to them.

I quietly enter Warren's room and crawl under the sheet next to him. I curl onto my side and watch the steady rise and fall of his chest. His hand shoots across the bed, a gurgled mumble pressing out of his lips. I move closer and wipe his brow. He's tacky to the touch. "You're okay, baby. Everything is okay, just sleep."

With more effort than it should take, he blinks his crusty lids open, voice rough and rattling. "You're a sight I've missed waking up to."

I smile for him, knowing it doesn't reach my eyes but trying all the same. "I made myself believe that I didn't miss the sight of you, Warren, but now that I've melted the ice from my heart, I can hardly believe I was talented enough to layer it on so thick."

He winces. "You can just say you missed me too. And you can also come here and kiss me."

I lace my fingers through his and lower my lips to a hair's breadth of his mouth. "I missed you. I love you. I'm going to kiss you a lot. And I'm sorry for hurting your heart and being the reason you're in pain right now."

He lifts his free hand to my cheek, rough fingers sliding over my skin, pushing back a mess of frizzy curls and tucking them behind my ear. "I'm willing to let you make all of it up to me. Just so long as you know you've had your say. Now it's my turn. You're mine, Tessa. I won't ever be without you again. Whatever comes, we stay together."

I move my lips against his, giving him the reassurance he needs and for the most part, meaning it. There's no one else for me outside of him, and while he's unable to defend himself I have no intention of leaving his side. When the time comes for me to leave him, I'll see to it that he's safe and happy in Marcie's arms.

I deepen our kiss, making sure he can feel my love. I need him to know that what I buried behind a wall of ice was never dead. Everything I've ever felt for him is still here. All it needed was a little fire to thaw it out.

His hands circle my waist and he tries to lift me onto him. I pull back. "Slow down, Gripr. You're not ready for more than just my apologies. I'm truly sorry for everything that's happened to you from the first moment that I stopped talking to you. Especially Chopper." I brush my hand along the scruff of Warren's jaw, his face still paler than it should be. "Chopper was a comfort to me when I ripped a hole in my soul. He meant a lot to me. But when I thought he killed you, I asked him to take me to you." A tear drips from my lashes. "I begged him to leave my body with yours because dead or alive, I didn't want to leave that mountain without you."

He runs a thumb under my eye. "I *hate* that you let Chopper put his hands on you and I'll never fully understand how you could cut me loose the way you did, but you didn't know what he was and as much as I hate to admit it, he loved you the way I do. That's why he didn't kill me, Tess. Gary gave the order but Chopper spared my life because of his love for you."

"Spared?" I gape. "He left you. And he might not have started the fire that nearly burned you alive but he had no guarantee that you'd get off that mountain alive even without the fire."

His fingers tighten to the point of bruising. "Chopper did have a guarantee. *You.* He knew I'd crawl down off that mountain missing all my limbs and both lungs. And he knew that when I did, I'd kill him. I hate to say that to you because I know you loved him and his death is hurting you, but I have a whole list of people who need to die and he's just one less name for me to check off."

I look away, a shudder fluttering through me. "If Chopper lived, I wouldn't let you kill him. I'm ashamed of saying that out loud but you're right about the love I have for him." I force myself to look into Warren's eyes. "It's not even half as much as I love you and it's wholly different. But if Chopper were alive today, I'd choose you, and fight for him to have the right to live in whatever peace he could find. Because if it weren't for me coming between you, the two of you would be happy and out living the best lives that you could imagine for yourselves."

Warren's fingers reposition. He hoists me onto him, clenching his jaw with the impact. "Fine, Tessa. You can be outraged over what he did to me and still care about him enough to piss me off. I'll allow it, because he's *dead*. I don't need to fight with you about him. Mourn him like you should, but do it while you're scrubbing your scent back into my skin because all I can smell now is the fire I thought I lost you in and all I can hear is the sound of you screaming. If it wasn't for that, my life would be pretty darn good right now."

~

It's going to be a while before Warren can test out all of his parts. From the way he winces every time he tries to put any amount of my weight on him and the sound of the gravely groan that snaps his teeth together when he moves, he knows that. I'd say his eagerness has less to do with me anyway, and more to do with the euphoria of being alive because mingled with the pain in his eyes, I see the fear. He doesn't trust me anymore. For good reason.

I brush my fingers along his muscled shoulder, thankful the medication Dr. Lafferty left makes him sleepy. He doesn't need to hurt himself in order to cover terrible memories with better ones. He needs to sleep, heal, and choose to make his skin smell like a woman who isn't me.

Me being okay with him moving on from us is yet another sign of how the years apart have changed us, none more than this last one. We're now as different to one another as we are familiar. Warren's words are all the same but doubt rides each one of them, and I'm just plain terrified of getting him hurt again. I'm so scared that if I thought I could leave Chief's house without Warren moving heaven and earth to come after me, I would. I'd slip out of this bed right now and go after Beth. But Warren would follow me and in his current condition, if Beth didn't get to him, the club would.

He pinches my chin between his thumb and forefinger, eyes still closed and breathing steady. "What are you up to, Tess?"

I draw my hand away from his shoulder, staying propped on my elbow beside him. "I'm just watching you sleep, and copping a couple of feels to make sure you're still breathing."

His puffy eyes blink open. "Keep running that one around the tree. You might catch the tail end of that lie but I know you, so before you go thinking those thoughts in your head are good ideas, let it sink in real deep that if you sneak out of this house while I'm sleeping, I'm going to hunt you down and make you the saddest woman alive for a very long time. Considering how you currently feel like you're already misery incarnate, I'd quit chasing tales around trees."

I swat his hand from my chin and sit up. "I wasn't thinking about running. I was thinking about how there are a lot of places in Hinton where Beth could be hiding and about how I know all of them."

"*We* know them." His groan turns into a cursing growl as he sits up next to me. "Every nook and cranny in this town has been explored by us, so Beth can't hide here and she knows it. That means if she's still here, she wants us to find her. Did you get ahold of your mom?"

I push his shoulders back to the mattress. "Chief doesn't want us making calls from here so he's taking care of warning her. I doubt Mom really wants to talk to me anyway, she'll blame me for what Chopper did. And Dr. Lafferty is going to blame me for you not following her orders. You need rest. You groan loud enough to break another rib every time I kiss you."

He snakes an arm around me. "Me voicing a little pain doesn't mean I can't handle it, and the doctor left plenty of pain medication. You can drug me up and rub yourself all over me, then you can make me another batch of that chicken soup you made earlier."

I raise a brow. "Soup that I *made*? It was canned, and Chief bought it for you, so I'll tell him you're grateful I know how to work his microwave."

Warren traces a finger over my cheek and down my neck. "I'm grateful for a lot of things, Tess. Like you being here every time I wake up. Patience was never your strong suit so I know this waiting is hard for you. But just give me a couple more days and then we'll go put a bullet in Beth's head *together*."

I run my fingers gently over his chest. His skin is littered with bruises and entire patches of his lean form are knotted and swollen. "You're going to need more than a couple of days, but I promise you, this is all going to end very soon."

His grip curves around the back of my neck. "I already know that, and I don't like the tone of your voice so knock it off. Where we go, what we do, and who *we* kill, we do it together. And while I'm laying down this law for you, let's go ahead and talk about the part where I'll break the neck of any man who gets near you again. Me and no one else, Tessa. Ever. Make me that oath and you keep it to your dying day because I'm keeping mine to you. If another man touches you, with your consent or not, I *will* kill him."

I look into his eyes, my own open wide so he can see the whole of my soul. "I made that oath on the first day I decided to start talking to you again, so don't pick fights with me when I already hate myself for making you watch anyone else put their hands on me. I'm yours, Warren. In life and in death, I belong to you."

His grip loosens, a little bit of that fear in his eyes subsiding. "I like the life part. Remind me how that goes again because you always were good at making up and I need you to put a little more effort into the apologies you've been trying to give me."

I move toward his mouth, the sound of the front door clicking closed catching my attention, right along with the two male voices falling into a whisper. I move away from Warren's clutching grip, his body pulling toward mine until he has no choice but to let go of me. "Tessa," he growls. "I need pants, and you need to stay put."

I point to the bedside table where his smoke-infused cargo pants are washed and folded. They're torn and most of what he had in his pockets is missing. "You can't stand up on your own, Warren, so you're staying here. Your knife is under my pillow. If anyone comes in this door, use it."

"No," he grinds, the bed creaking under his weight as he does exactly what I just told him not to.

I open the thin slab separating us from the rest of the house and slip into the hallway, narrowing my gaze on him. "Get back in that bed. I'll see who this is and I'll do what needs doing. On my own."

~6~

The lack of pants and the closed bedroom door should slow Warren down long enough for me to see who is in the house. I just hope I'm fast enough to draw them outside and away from him before he makes a potentially nude appearance. The kitchen is ahead of me at the end of the short hallway. I tread softly over the tile and listen at the archway leading from the kitchen into the living room. "Are you sure she's dead?" Chief's whisper crawls out of his throat.

The other male scoffs. "She's got makeup on so I can't say what shade of dead she is, but the caved-in skull and maggot eyes seemed pretty final to me."

My spine goes rigid, legs stiffening. Chief growls a curse. "How am I going to tell Tessa about this?"

I pick up my lead-filled feet and force the heavy weight of my body forward. "Easy, Chief. Just open your mouth and let the words fly. Who is it that's dead this time?"

Chief's head jerks in my direction, mouth falling open and a shot of fear darting through his eyes.

Deputy Durand does a double take, hat clutched tightly in his hand where he stands huddled in the entryway with Chief. The latter rolls up his jaw and coaxes a single word out of his lips. "Tessa…"

I clear my throat. "Try again. My name is Tessa and I'm still kicking. Whose ticket got punched? Beth's? Did my sister get her one-way ride out of this town?"

Chief drags a hand across his mouth, scrubbing it as if to grease the wheels so he can let loose of the words his tongue is holding. He walks toward me, motioning to his couch. "Here, honey. Let's sit down and talk for a minute."

My skin pricks. "I don't need to sit. Just spit out your words." I look past him to Deputy Durand. "If not my sister, then whose skull is caved in?"

Durand stares at me, a mix of pity and anger plastered on his pale face. He's one of the few men in the department who doesn't frequent the Grille. I always took his straitlaced ways to mean he was a coward. Men who starch their collars so stiffly usually are. It's easier to hide behind the pretense of righteousness than to have to get your hands dirty.

I step past Chief and toward Durand, using the motion to hide the unease rustling through my limbs. "You're not happy to see me and I can assure you the feeling is mutual. We can take that up with Chief later because he's the one who let both of us into his house. Right now, we need to deal with you naming the name of the dead. *Who* is she?"

He takes a step forward to match my own. "Chief is trying to tell you. Have a seat."

"No--"

"Just come here, Tessa." Chief grips my arm, cutting off my protest.

Warren slides around the corner, flipping his knife through his fingers. "You're going to want to remove your hand, or you're going to lose it."

Durand draws his gun and Warren laughs. Chief turns me loose and waves his hands out to either side of him. "Stop it! Both of you. We don't need guns and knives. We need to sit down and talk this through because Durand just found Rose Marie and what happened to her wasn't done by bikers or thieves."

My body goes slack. Two sets of arms wrap around me, Warren's two bands of flaming iron, his grunt a poor excuse for a warning as he rips me from Chief's embrace and drops us both to the cushioned seat Chief had been trying to get me onto all along. My lips flutter. "Mom?"

Chief shuffles down into a crouch, resting a gentle hand on my knee. "Yeah, honey. Your mom is dead."

"How?" Warren asks the question my own lips are too shocked to ask.

Chief wipes a hand down his face. "After what you two said about Beth, I made getting a hold of Rose Marie a top priority but she wasn't answering her phone, and the two times I went by there, no one answered the door."

Warren smacks Chief's hand off my knee. "That doesn't sound like priority. That sounds like you doing the bare minimum."

Chief straightens, hooking his thumbs through his belt and glaring down at Warren. "What would you have had me do? Huh? I saw Rose Marie right after things blew up at the Grille. I doubted Tessa would go there, and the club must have doubted it too because Rose Marie said she hadn't seen any of you. Beth, Arnold, and some of the other family members were gathered with her at that time, because Rose Marie was destroyed over the death of her husband."

"So you left her in their capable hands?" Warren snaps.

A vein pops on the side of Chief's neck. "I had no reason not to, and I had more pressing matters at the time. Rose Marie talked about needing to get away from the press so when I went back and she didn't answer, I thought maybe she did leave. That maybe Beth and Arnold went with her. Half the citizens of this town ran off after that shootout at the Grille and the other half started packing when the mountain started burning!"

Warren jabs a finger up at him. "The first time you couldn't get Rose Marie on the phone, you should have busted in her door. You didn't do it because you're too stupid to see what Beth is painting right in front of all our faces. That's why she keeps killing. Rose Marie's blood is on *your* hands."

I grip Warren's leg, the scratch of his cargo pants a welcome relief. He's brazen enough to be naked in front of these men but we're going to be here a while. I need the details of my mom's death. For everything Beth has done, I can't see her taking the life of our mother. If she did, I need to know, so when I'm ending her life, I can recount the full tally of Beth's sins. "Chief, you haven't believed a word of what we told you about Beth. My mom's death changed that?"

Chief's shoulders sag. "I can't fathom who else would do to her what Deputy Durand says was done."

I look at the deputy, whose eyes are still locked on Warren. "What happened to Rose Marie?"

Deputy Durand breaks his stare away from Warren and moves to the center of the room. "Chief briefed me on the information you gave him, including the suspicion about your sister. With the state police and FBI crawling around, we decided to keep her name out of the official record." His eyes dart to Warren. "Without evidence, our hands are tied."

"Tied is better than being cut off," Warren smirks.

I nudge his side gently enough for him to get the message. He readjusts, curling an arm around my shoulder. He flicks his hand at Durand. "Go on, get to the part where you tell her how those tied hands of yours got her mom killed."

Durand widens his stance. "We didn't get anyone killed, the Leidolf did. The added media coverage they brought in and the dead bodies spread everywhere only jammed us up even more. The FBI is classifying most of the deaths as gang violence." His eyes dip to mine, face softening a fraction. "What I saw inside your mom's place wasn't violence. It's evil. Pure evil."

I clasp my hands together, trying to put up the same front Warren is, pretending nothing is fazing me, but he knows better than to believe me. He shifts closer, arm tightening and lips moving to my ear. "I'm sorry, baby."

I lean into him, focus still on Durand. "It doesn't sound like this ends with only a crushed skull. What else did you see?"

His throat works, eyes shifting to Chief's for approval. Chief unhooks his thumbs and paces to his recliner, plopping into it with a heavy sigh. "Go ahead, tell her everything you told me."

Durand lowers his gaze to the floor, jaw clenched tight on a breath before he looks back at me. "Chief sent me over to Rose Marie's with the go-ahead to enter the home if she didn't answer the door or phone again. She didn't, so I broke a glass pane on the front door and gained entry. Right away, I could smell death. At this point, I'm pretty good at picking up on the scent of decay." He shifts. "There's blood splatter all over what I assume is your mom's bedroom. The bed is made but there's a bulge in the center of it. I carefully pulled back the covers and found," his throat works, "pictures of you. Nude ones. They were spread all over pillows that were soaked in blood, the pillows being the bulge I'd seen."

Warren curses, his protective arms tightening like a vice. "I know right where she got those pictures, that lying, evil, son of a——"

I dig my nails into his leg, eyes trained on Durand. "You didn't find Rose Marie in the bed?"

His head gives a sad shake. "I cleared each room of the house. There wasn't blood anywhere but in that room. No drag marks, no drops, and nothing seemed out of place. The house was clean and neat as a pin. Instead of it being a crime scene, I started thinking that maybe it was another staged scene, like the one at your house with the blood being pig instead of human." He swallows. "Then I went out onto a little porch at the back of the house. It's enclosed and just barely big enough to fit the dresser and daybed that are inside it."

Warren lets out another string of profanities. "Tessa knows the place. That drafty porch was her sorry excuse for a bedroom and it was the only *tidy* room in that house."

Durand frowns. "I thought that might end up being the case because Rose Marie wasn't killed in that room but her body was there, in plain sight, staged on that daybed."

My voice breaks. "Staged how?"

His head tilts, voice softening as he regards me. "As I said, your mom appears to have died in her own bedroom. Then she was cleaned up, moved into your room, and dressed in a white gown she wasn't wearing when she was killed because there's no blood on it. And...even though there's not much left of her face that even resembles a face anymore, someone went through a lot of trouble to put makeup on her."

My stomach rolls. I press a hand to it and close my eyes.

"There's more," Durand continues. "Tessa, there's a crown on her head and a sash across her shoulders. I think it's from a pageant I seem to recall you winning when you were a teen."

Warren speaks for the benefit of the other men in the room but I can feel his eyes boring into the side of my face. He wants me to fear Beth because if I do, I won't go after her on my own. "Beth is taking the death of her dad out on Tessa. She took Gary's life and now Rose Marie's, the dress-up being her confession because she's past thrill-killing. She wants Tessa to know who the murderer is. She wants Tessa to see how easy it is for the life to be drained from everyone Tessa cares about."

Durand walks toward us. I open my eyes and meet his. His frown deepens. "We didn't want to convict your sister before we knew the truth and I'm still not convinced she could do the things I've seen but... Tessa, you probably don't remember me from your younger days. I'm a bit older than you, but I'm only a couple of years older than Beth. I dated her for a little bit. Just a few months or so. We broke up because when we'd...*fool around*, she'd ask me to call her Tessa. At first, I thought she was kidding. When I realized she wasn't, I didn't see her again. I'd forgotten all about that happening until Chief came to me with his suspicions about her. I'm no psychologist, but I think it's possible she had something wrong with her back then. Something wrong enough that it blistered into killing. I don't see why anyone but her would pose your mom up like that. The crime scene is targeted at you."

Warren shoves to his feet, the groan accompanying his pain turning menacing. "Of course it was. Because Beth was born wrong and she can't stand that Tessa is all kinds of right. But this woman sitting here is the reason the sun gets up in the morning and vengeance for all of these murders belongs to her, so don't worry about evidence and those tied hands of yours. I'm the hammer of Tessa's justice. I'll mete out the retribution while you two coppers go twiddle your dee's and stay *dumb*." He reaches a hand down to me. "The demon formerly known as Beth isn't going to have the luxury of prison, and anyone standing between her and me is going to share in her fate."

~7~

I watch steam rise from the pot of boiling water where the macaroni is cooking. Durand is gone. He left when Warren ushered me out of the living room so I could release my sorrow in private. I did that, laying myself bare in Warren's solid arms until sleep took us both. I wish I could say that I woke with more resolve. Different resolve. Anything that would add strength to the fight inside me, but I didn't. I woke to Dr. Lafferty's knock on our door and a rope of guilt pulled tight around my neck.

Even when I was fighting Warren with every ounce of strength I had within myself, he kept all of his promises to me. It didn't matter to him if I knew he was or not, he did it because he loves me. And even after all the damage I've caused, he loves me still. I'm ashamed that he does. Ashamed that I let him get close to me again because if I hadn't, he could have had a chance at breaking our bond. Instead, he's here, still putting me first, above even his own life. He knows Beth is messing with me and there's no imagination needed to guess who she'll come for. The only question is when. If she gets to Warren now, his will be the next body I'm made to find.

And that's what Beth wants, for me to find them. That's why she cleaned up Mom's house and got rid of any blood outside of Mom's bedroom. People stopping by wouldn't see anything amiss from a window and if I'd gone there, I would have to live with the visual of our dead mother painted up like one of Beth's dolls in what used to be my bed.

Warren isn't the only man whose future I'm guilt-ridden over. Despite Chief's disdain for Warren and his barbed accusations, I owe him more than the disrespect I've been heaping on him. "I'm sorry about showing myself to Durand. I should have stayed hidden and waited for you to finish hearing what he had to say."

Chief taps his fingers on the island where he's sitting and watching me do my best imitation of cooking. "Durand knew I had you holed up somewhere from the second you hung up on me. I had him cover for me so I could sneak away. I wasn't about to tell him I brought you here or that I let that mutt of yours come with you, but we can trust Durand. If I say your whereabouts are unknown, they're unknown."

I stir the macaroni. "Let him know Warren and I won't forget our appreciation of his forgetfulness."

Chief groans. "Durand isn't looking to garner favor with either of you. He hightailed it out of here because he wants no part of my houseguests, and I don't blame him. We need to consider what's going to happen if you two are found here. Everything I've said and done will be questioned and all it will take is one good lawyer to spin this and make it look like the two of you set Beth up. Her reputation in town is pretty pristine compared to both of you, and I'm with Durand when it comes to not fully believing Beth could be capable of doing the things I've seen."

I drop the slotted spoon onto the counter. "You don't think Beth is capable but you think I am? That Warren is?"

Chief's chin thrusts toward his bedroom. "I wouldn't put anything past that one in there, but no, Tessa, I don't think you're bloodthirsty enough to slice women open and remove their organs. I don't believe your sister could do a thing like that either but with what you've told me lately and what Durand found in your momma's house, my judgment just might well be off on both of you."

I flatten my palms on the island in front of him. "You better hope you start judging Beth right because at the rate she's been killing lately, you go soft on her and she's liable to slit your throat before you can reconsider."

He leans away from me. "I'm not going soft. I already sent Durand back over to Rose Marie's. He called it in like he just found her dead while out doing a routine check. He'll say the glass on the door was already broken so he took that as cause to enter. This way we have an official report and a reason to have the whole department hunting for Beth. Between us, the state police, and the FBI, she won't be in the wind too much longer. But we don't have a lot to go on with liking her for the other murders, especially with Matt Honaker dead. She tied that bow up neat enough that if all this serial killer duo speculation is true, we better hope that when we pick her up, her story has holes in it. Because she'll be singing a tune that points anywhere but at her and if she has a shred of proof to go with that tune, we're all getting burned."

Warren coughs, drawing our attention to where he's leaning on the wall, arms crossed over his chiseled chest, taking on a posture that's hiding how hard it is for him to stand up and breathe at the same time. "Don't you worry your pretty little head, Chief. Beth isn't going to live long enough to sing any ballads."

Chief jabs a finger in his direction. "Yeah, you go right ahead and keep telling me how much of a killer you are. If it weren't for Tessa, I'd already have you locked up and I'd be out burying the key right now."

I tramp to Warren's position and slip my arm around him so he can lean on me instead of the wall. He curls his arm around me and presses a kiss to the top of my head. "Thanks for keeping me out of jail, baby."

I sigh. "Chief, I already told you who is responsible for the murders and there's no point in the three of us tearing at each other's throats. What's done is done and what isn't will be. Just tell Durand to keep running cover for you and if anyone should stumble upon Warren and me, we'll all stick to the story that we broke in of our own accord and you were none the wiser."

Chief pushes out of his chair. "There are too many cooks in the kitchen, Tessa, so at least a few of them will be suspicious. Law enforcement is already pointing fingers at each other every time a body is found, namely at me, because no one wants to take the blame for dropping the ball on this town. Heck, the majority of the people still think the bikers are the trouble even though I keep telling them the Leidolf are only half of it, and I'm not so sure they're the worst half."

I walk Warren to the counter, letting him rest his weight against it while I turn off the stove. "Montrose's followers are the bad half but the wolves who deserve to be called Leidolf will take care of them, and I'll take care of Beth. Just tell all those do-gooders that while they're busy pointing fingers, they should also keep an eye on the innocent citizens so Beth doesn't get to them before I get to her."

Chief walks around the island and places a hand on my shoulder. "Honey, you're a tough girl but this callous attitude isn't you. Taking someone's life, even someone who deserves it, should never be a choice you let yourself make."

Warren snorts on a laugh. "Taking out the trash is a common courtesy and Beth is stinking up the town." He snakes an arm around my waist and pulls me out from under Chief's touch. "Not everyone is callous enough to do what needs to be done but me and my woman don't have that problem. We'll be putting Beth's bag of bones out in the dump where she belongs. You're welcome."

Spit gathers in the corners of Chief's mouth. "No one asked for your opinion. And if you knew what was good for you, instead of being here influencing this girl, you'd tuck your tail and run like the rest of the dogs did. No one has seen hide nor hair of them since the night those cowards set fire to my town and if you weren't hurt and playing on Tessa's sympathies, you'd be gone too." His eyes bore into mine. "Let that sink in for you. None of them are here because they got what they needed from you, and he'll be gone just as soon as he gets it too."

"Not true," Warren corrects, the grin in his voice stoking my compassion for Chief. "You're seeing the most *special* wolf right here in your house, and my hide sure does appreciate the red-carpet treatment. Though I'd appreciate it a little more if the next time you buy my groceries, you'd throw in a couple of steaks. Tessa's plain macaroni is getting old." He nuzzles my neck. "Unlike her attitude. This callousness of hers is coming along just fine, and it's darn sexy."

Chief storms from the room. I bump Warren's face out of my neck and spin in his arms, facing him. "Was that necessary?"

He rests his forehead on mine, leaning more of his weight against the counter. "It was."

Dr. Lafferty treads her way across the floor. "Sorry to interrupt, and believe me, I don't want to be involved with any of this more than I already am, that includes hearing about murder plots. But is what Chief Dunbar just said true? The club is gone? The Leidolf are no longer in Hinton?"

I huff out a humorless laugh but before I can tell her that it's unlikely, Chief stomps back into the room, neck flaming red and chest puffing. "I forgot you were here, Dr. Lafferty."

She tugs her bag over her shoulder. "I was just on my way out, but after Warren didn't listen to me, he left the door open so I heard most of the conversation the three of you were having. I won't repeat any of it but it is bothering me. I was just asking them if it's true that the club is gone?"

His lip curls in Warren's direction. "None of them have been in or out of Riverside Grille. It was abandoned the night of their shootout. I went by and had myself a look at Town's End, too. That place is almost as much of a ghost town as the Grille, but the cowards seemed to leave there in enough of a hurry to forget some bikes. I impounded quite a few of them just this morning."

Warren rubs his cheek along mine, continuing to poke Chief by marking his territory right in front of the lawman. "Those bikes he's talking about are all mine, baby. And all legal. I'm looking forward to getting you on the back of every single one of them." He brushes his lips against my skin and lifts his eyes to Chief. "Just like at the Grille, you won't find anything incriminating at my place either, because the Leidolf are smarter than you. They wouldn't have left even the bikes of our dead brothers sitting around. And if I was a betting man, which I am, I'd say more than one wolf watched you scouring the place. When I see my brothers again, I'll be sure to pass on your sentiments. Without Chopper around, I'm curious as to how the others will decide to make you eat that name you just called us. The Leidolf are not cowards."

Chief clamps his thumbs behind his belt. "The only wolves left in this town are *dead* ones, and a lone wolf who is half on his way. So you go right ahead and talk to anyone you want because I'm tearing your life apart and sifting through the pile of tales you keep telling. When I get to the truth, you better hope the good Lord gets to you before I do." His head ticks. "Come on, Doctor. I'll walk you out. Your patient looks well enough to me that you won't need to come back."

Dr. Lafferty moves to Warren's side and digs through her bag, placing a satchel on the counter next to us. "Despite you being a terrible patient, your lungs are sounding better and your other wounds are healing about as well as can be expected under these circumstances, so you should be fine on your own for a while. I left a supply of medication and bandages in the bedroom and here are the extras." She nudges the satchel and gives me a sad smile. "See to it that his burns are cared for, make sure he's eating and staying hydrated, and he really should be fine."

I nod. "I'll take care of him. And...on that other thing. If I believed any of what I just heard, I'd make my lone wolf go to a hospital."

She hesitates, clarity drawing her lips into a frown. "Thank you for that. I'll keep waiting. Just... Well, I don't even live in Hinton but what's happening here is affecting everyone. People are worried the evil will seep out. Don't let that happen. Whether it's your sister or not, don't let anything escape." She tips my pot of overcooked macaroni toward her and then pats Warren's cheek. "You two be careful, and come see me when you can. I'll make you a steak dinner."

Warren

If I focus on the pain I'm in, I can't move. Not even to breathe. There isn't an inch of me that isn't hurting, from the bottoms of my feet to all those little places inside me that I couldn't name even if I did know anything about anatomy. I have to take shallow breaths and talk slower, faking my way through the appearance of being better than I am until I make it out of this nightmare and into the next one.

There are no delusions on my part about how long it's going to be before life feels anything close to normal. Putting an end to Beth doesn't stop the war, she's only one battle. The rest will come in time. Brother against brother and wolf against imposters wearing the label. I'm only hoping the club comes for us later rather than sooner. I'm still spitting up blood, and still hiding it from Tessa.

A coughing spell doubles me over, bloody phlegm drawing up my sore throat. I swallow the nasty loogie back down. If Tessa wasn't next to me, I'd spit the bloody mass into the soda bottle I emptied and hid between the mattress and the headboard. I'd rather have her right where she is, though, and swallowing this junk back down is no less gross than stomaching this uncheesed macaroni she likes.

She rubs my back. "You keep saying the cough is getting better but it doesn't sound like it."

I paint my face in a mask meant to hide my pain and snake my arm around her for good measure, pulling her to my chest where I'm close to those lips I've missed so much. "You think my scratchy voice is sexy so I'm just keeping my throat raw for you."

She sighs. "This is serious, Warren. Dr. Lafferty will come back if I ask her to, but Chief isn't giving us a phone for a reason. So be honest with me. Either you're feeling good enough to move in a few days, if Chief even gives us that long, or I need to leave you here and hunt down a phone. You remember Jimmy's number, right?"

I smooth my fingers over her mess of soft hair. It sticks out like she's been fighting with a thorn bush but it feels like silk. "I'm as antsy as you are but not much can be done about it right now." I leave off telling her that with the way my left knee is grinding, I wasn't sure I'd even make it back to this bedroom. Every move I make requires me to dig deep into my well of resolve, what that well lacks being made up by the pain medication Dr. Lafferty is so generously supplying. "You have that look about you, Tess. The one that tells me you're getting ready to do something stupid. Don't. Because I don't want to have to make you regret it."

Before she can tell me she's not thinking about doing what I know she is, I press my lips to hers, the motion feeling so right that I have a twinge of guilt over Marcie. I pursued her, whispered things in her ear to convince even myself that Tessa's lips weren't the only ones mine wanted to mold to.

I break from the sweet caress of Tessa's lips and study every inch of the face that feels like home. The one I used to see in my mind's eye whenever I lied to Marcie. "I'll be ready to move in a few days and Chief can bellyache all he wants but he won't kick us out. He's too busy pumping you for information because his panties are in a bunch over me being the one to figure out who his murderer is. He's too pathetic to ask me questions himself."

Tessa leans onto her elbow. "Maybe so, but he's still sticking his neck out for us and Chief knows we're a package deal, so stop spreading your testosterone around."

I knock her elbow loose and flip her on top of me, choking down the stab of pain. "That man has never liked me and he's liked us being together even less. That's a problem for me. Especially now that he's creeping around here whispering in your ear. I don't trust you. I love the heck out of you but I don't trust you one little bit. So if you don't want me winding him up, you better give me something else to spread around because one way or another, I'm going to make you remember your place, and Chief is going to know his too."

Her eyes bore into mine, confronting the pain I can't tame. "My *place* is to be out there killing my sister but instead of hunting her, I'm here with you, so you don't forget *your* place. And stop acting like a baby over Chief icing you out. I tell you every little detail of what he says to me."

I tap her temple. "Yeah, but you don't tell me every little detail of what you're up to, and it would serve you to run all of your thoughts by me because I'm in my place, Tessa." I grip her chin between my fingers. "*You* are not going *anywhere* without *me*. We'll find Beth together, and that starts with Arnold. I heard Chief tell you that Arnold gave him the slip. That means he's with Beth. He probably knows she's been killing people but kept his mouth shut because he loves her. I don't know why, other than the fact that he's an idiot, but it's obvious he loves her by the way that he looks at her. I know, because it's the same way I look at you. Even when you're all mad and murdery."

Her jaw grinds, those high cheekbones looking like they can slice me open. I grin, removing my fingers from her chin but staying my course. "If you're not going to get naked, feed me another bite of that disgusting macaroni because the stench of pig is so strong in here, I wouldn't enjoy a steak even if I did have one."

She digs her fingers into my dimples and forcibly removes my grin. "And here I was about to go out and get you a ribeye."

I cup my hands around her backside and dig my fingers into her until she releases my mouth. "No, you were about to run off to go find Beth on your own. That's why I'm reminding you that your place is wherever I am. If I'm in this bed, so are you. If I walk down the hall, so do you. You don't leave this house until I do. We hunt Beth down *together*. Then you look away while I kill her because I'm not letting you do that. Ending her life will haunt you but wiping that witch off the face of the earth won't bother me one little bit. I'll do it with a smile on my lips and a song in my heart."

She wriggles to get free and I loosen my grip, but only because it hurts like hell to have her moving like that. She crawls off me. "It's the people Beth murdered who are going to haunt me. But Beth isn't the only problem we have. If the Leidolf are laying low enough for no one to even know *one* of them is still here, then it's only because both charters are more interested in hunting us than each other."

I look toward the window. Beyond it is the backyard, a place where the club could be watching us from right now. "Like I told Chief, the bikes he found are probably all mine. I had quite a few stored around the garage and down at the house, and the club has men in charge of moving things that need to be moved. They left my things because they figure I might go for them, so they're watching the garage. Or were. Now that Chief raided the place, they might guess I'll stay away."

She sighs, drawing my attention back to the sorrow and worry that are permanent fixtures on her face. "So you think they know you're alive? What about me? Chopper? Gary?"

I press a hand to her cheek, comforted by the fact that even though she's angry with me, she's still right next to me. "No matter what side they're on, I imagine every wolf is well informed on Gary's death and probably knows Chopper is gone too because the war popping off didn't scatter them. It would make them fall in closer together, stick to protocols and contingencies, things I'd have no idea about if I hadn't joined up when I did."

I lower my hand and think back to my short-lived run as part of the Hinton Charter. The men brought me into their fold and I betrayed them, same as Tessa did. I'm still Leidolf, though. It was clear to me when I took my oath that once I was in, I was in for life. That's why Gary ordered my life to end. I stole his prize possession and after the way Tessa fought for Chopper, he wasn't going to let her fight for me because I was more of a threat to him than Chopper ever could be. Chopper had personal loyalty to Gary, something that went above his place in the Leidolf as Gary's second.

My first loyalty lies with Tessa and Gary was making decisions that hurt her, and he knew I'd make her and everyone else see the truth of that.

"I was brought up to speed on a lot of things real fast, Tess. The Leidolf are smart enough to know how to blend in and with all of the new faces in town, no one is going to notice a cleaned-up wolf. All the guys have to do is take off the kutte and ditch the bike, and then they're just another person in the crowd. Why do you think most of them only have tattoos in places easily hidden by casual clothing?"

She glances down to where my wolf is hidden by my pants. "With Gary and Chopper gone, I'm not valuable to Montrose's charter anymore. I still betrayed the others, but for them to come after us before going after the strays only makes sense if it's you they're after. Why would they be so determined to kill you?"

I slide my hand to the back of her neck and urge her toward me. "Baby, you're still the prize. Montrose's strays capturing you is a slap in the face of the Hinton Charter. That alone would have both sides hunting you. Then there are your betrayals. Whether you meant to or not, you hurt our club. On top of the personal affronts, you did things that could have brought down the entire organization. That's why *all* of the wolves are still gunning for you." I press my lips to her nose. "I don't know what type of accountability the club will demand now that Gary and Chopper are gone, but I do know that *they* know I won't let you be hurt, so my neck is out there just as much as Chief's is. Promise me you won't run off and do something stupid that gets it chopped off."

She runs her fingers through the increasing scruff of my jaw. "I promise that everything I do from this day forward will only be with the intention of keeping you from being hurt."

My fingers tighten on the back of her neck and I pull her lips down to mine. "You're talking in riddles but I can read between those lines, sweetheart. You're not doing anything I don't approve of, and I can promise you that I don't approve of anything you're thinking about right now." I part her lips and kiss her deeply, the ache of worry in my chest easing when her body conforms to mine, her kiss as genuine and as full of love as my own.

I drag my hand down her back and over her thigh, tugging her leg over me, ready to attempt getting these clothes off of her one more time. The bedroom door bangs open, slamming against the wall with a thud barely heard above the screech of my name.

Tessa hits the floor, head colliding with the oversized nightstand. I jerk upright, getting my arms out in front of me just in time to catch Marcie's soaring body. She jumped at me from halfway across the room, the impact crunching my ribs and slamming my head back against the headboard. I yell out a growling curse.

"Warren!" My name screeches from her lips again, her mouth probing every inch of my face. "I thought you were dead. Oh, babe, I thought you were gone but you're not and here you are. I love you so much, Warren. I love you so much and I'm here to get you out of this place."

My eyes fling to Tessa's. They're wide and dark, focused on the woman whose knees are clamped around my thighs. Marcie's mouth covers mine and Tessa moves for the door. I peel Marcie away. "Wait."

Marcie slows her groping but it wasn't her I was talking to. Tessa stops at the threshold, her body turning so she's facing me. Marcie buries herself in my neck, her lips working overtime to both kiss and cry while she professes her love over and over. I pull her to me, holding her tight against my chest to try to get her to stop wiggling around while I stare into Tessa's eyes.

"Don't go." I want the words to be an order but with Marcie in my arms, it's more pleading than final. I tighten my arms around Marcie even more, as if doing so can keep Tessa in place, but I'm not asking her to stay in this room anymore and she can feel that in what's passing between us. I need time with Marcie. Alone. I owe her that much. I press my lips to her head, eyes only for Tessa. "Wait for me. Just wait for me."

~9~

Tessa

Warren's been locked in the bedroom with Marcie for hours. I want to be sore about it but I can't. I've done him so wrong that he can do almost anything to me and still not get close to the damage I've caused. Marcie is better for him anyway. Good, sweet, kind, never-do-you-wrong Marcie is who he deserves. She wouldn't dream of doing the things I've done and she doesn't have the type of connections that are bad for Warren's health. No one is going to target him because of her. With Marcie, Warren has a future. That's why I should just go, run away from here instead of waiting like he asked me to. I don't want him to have a part in killing Beth anyway. I don't want him to be a part of any of this.

"I'm sorry," Chief mutters from his recliner. He's been sitting there staring at me for about as long as I've been contemplating running out that front door.

"You're not," I answer, sitting on the couch across from him. "You're tickled pink that Warren's with Marcie and not me. That's why you called her here. I'm not mad at you for it, but I do want to know why you hate him so much. Did Warren find out about your little secret before I did?"

Chief sits forward and rests his elbows on his knees. "No. You're the only person who has dirt on me that's wet enough to make a mess of my life. I don't like Warren for other reasons."

I mimic his posture. "Which are? For as long as I can remember, you've treated him badly and I know it isn't because he's poor or from the wrong side of town because there's only one side to this town. So if Warren doesn't know things about you that he shouldn't, why are you so dead set against him?"

"Why are you so dead set on being with him?" Chief counters.

I pick myself up off my knees and lean back against the couch. "I fell in love with Warren before I was old enough to write my name and as hard as I've fought that love, it's never left me. I could force myself to stop thinking about him but whenever I'd see his face, all the old feelings would surge up and break my heart all over again. Now it's your turn. Answer my question. And don't get confused here, Chief. I'm not asking you out of jealousy. I know Marcie is better than me and that she's the right choice for Warren. I have no intention of breaking them up. I just want to know what makes you hate him as much as you do."

Chief watches me. "Maybe you don't have any intention of breaking them up, Tessa, but does Warren? Because I didn't call her here to hurt you. The more people knowing who's in my house the worse this is for all of us, and there's nothing quite as bad as a scorned lover. But he doesn't need to be here sleeping in my bed and Marcie can get him out of here. I told her to take him out of town, which should make you happy. She'll get him to someplace safe."

My eyes narrow. "There is no place that's safe. Not yet. I intend to fix that for him and then you can pretend Marcie was his hero and puff her up about that, but getting Warren someplace safe wasn't why you called her. Tell me why Warren itches your skin bad enough that you ratted yourself out to his girlfriend?"

"At least you know *you're* not his girlfriend," Chief deflects, looking down at his hands. "When I was a young man, Warren's momma was *my* girlfriend. All through school and up until the year after graduation."

My breath catches. "Like Warren and me."

He nods. "Just about."

I sit forward again. "You know I'm good at math, right? I know how old you are and I know when Warren was born. He's your son?"

Chief jumps to his feet. "Heck, no! I wouldn't have done him like that, Tessa. You know yourself that I take care of my kids. I support Erin and my son with her the same way I support my wife and boys."

I shrug. "I know you do that now, but you're talking about a time when you were a lot younger."

He shoves his hands through his hair. "Warren's not my kid. He belongs to that no good filthy father of his. That dirtbag swooped in on my Annabelle right after I left for the academy. Before I made it through training, she was knocked up and breaking off our engagement. Then I had to come back here and spend these years watching her drink herself to death." His nostrils flare. "I've hated that boy of hers because if it wasn't for him, I could have gotten Annabelle away from that filth she married."

I stare at him, the anger he still harbors painting a picture Warren and I know all too well. "You loved her. All this time, you've loved her."

Chief takes a step back and brushes a hand over his eyes. "I've never loved anything the way I loved that woman, and seeing her waste away like she did... Having to arrest her and hear the stories of what she'd do with men in town for a drink..." His fists clench. "Life is full of pain and regret, Tessa, and all I ever wanted to do was save you from becoming what my Annabelle became."

Emotion swirls in my gut. Chief lost the love of his life to someone who ruined her. Just like I let Matt ruin me...after I ruined Warren.

I get off the couch and stand in front of Chief, slipping my hands into his and holding him tight. "Watching Warren and me grow up, as tight as you and Annabelle were, must have stirred your memories something awful. They must have stirred hers too because a mother has never hated a son's girlfriend any more than Annabelle despised me. I'm sorry that me loving Warren caused that kind of pain for both of you, and I appreciate that you've always looked out for me, but Warren didn't choose his parents and he's nothing like either of them. Same as I'm nothing like either of mine."

Chief inhales a ragged breath. "We all get something from our parents. You look just like that pretty momma of yours, and Warren looks just like that serpent father of his."

"Something else we didn't choose. We didn't have any control over what we were born with or born into."

Chief drops my hands with a heavy sigh. "I know, and I've scolded myself plenty over the years, so I don't need you to heap coals on my head. I've watched that boy grow up and found fault even in the way he walks, but deep down I know he isn't close to being the belly crawler his sperm donor is. I just can't bring myself to like him, though. I can't, Tessa. And despite my prejudice against him, I don't think I'm wrong in you being better off without him."

"Were you better off without Annabelle?"

Chief's face falls, his ears red and his eyes dodging mine. "Chief," I whisper. "If Warren had a choice, he would have chosen to be yours. I wish Annabelle would have let *both* of you have that choice."

He sniffs, wiping at his eyes. "Yeah, well, she had it in her head that she had to marry the father of her baby. I told her I didn't care that people would know it wasn't mine, because of the timing of the baby and me being gone off to the academy, but she said she loved that man and that he wanted them to be a family." Chief's jaw works. "Some family they turned out to be."

I nod. "Yeah, that sums up how Warren feels about it too."

Chief meets my stare, his watery eyes softening. "I know what you must think of me because of my affair with Erin, but I do care for her. I care for my wife, my kids, and I've tried to do right by everyone. It's just that I can't bring myself to love my wife or Erin the way that I loved Annabelle. True heartbreak is something powerful, Tessa, and I'm sorry if I'm facilitating that in your life. I don't want to see you hurt, especially by me. But I do see history repeating itself, and some things should never be done twice."

I glance toward the back of the house where Warren is holed up with Marcie. "The part you have wrong is that this time around, it's the female who is the serpent. So have this conversation with Warren and get through his thick skull that he's the one who needs to do the staying away." I turn back to Chief. "I'm not good for you either and I'm sorry for that. You hold a special place in my heart and I feel better knowing that a man can find happiness in his life even when he can't love the woman in it the way he loved the first girl who caught his eye. Warren will be happy with Marcie."

Chief tucks his hands into his pockets. "It'll take you both some time, but you'll move on. You already proved that you know how."

I snort. "Yeah, I moved on with a rapist who joined my sister's serial killer cult. Thanks for reminding me. You're just the gift that keeps giving, Chief."

"Tessa," Marcie announces from the hallway I just turned away from. "Warren said for you to come. He wants to talk to you."

I lock eyes with Chief, surer now than I was before that what I'm thinking is the right choice. I don't bother turning around. "He only wants to know that I'm still in the house. Tell Warren that I'm holding a vigil right here in this living room. The door he's about to hear is only Chief leaving to rendezvous with his pointless task force."

Chief stomps past me and picks up his keys. "I think I make my points real clear. Like how if some woman wants to climb that dog in there like he's a new toy at the playground, she'll do it in her own bed."

I face him. He's glaring at Marcie. "Go on. You have thirty minutes, then I want him out of my house. That's the whole reason I told you to come with a full tank of gas."

Her hands fall to her sides and she spins on her heel, racing back to the bedroom. Chief opens the front door. "It's a good thing I know what it looks like when a suspect is getting ready to run, or else I would have just thought you were insulting me again." He nods to the door. "Ladies first."

~10~

Warren

I push off the bed. I knew sending Marcie for Tessa was a bad idea before I even did it, but the front of me is streaked in mascara and every bone in my body aches from the full weight of the sorrow Marcie unleashed on me. Chief called her here with a mouthful of lies, giving her hope that I was the one asking for her. She ran in here the way she did because she thought it was her name I was calling in the height of my pain. But I've had few thoughts of Marcie lately and I'm tired of Chief's overdone interest in Tessa.

When he first started singling her out, we were just kids and I was used to being hassled by adults so I didn't pay too much attention to the way he'd cut me down and lift her up. I agreed with his lifting and let the rest roll off my back. Then I grew up. Once I realized Chief's intention was to keep Tessa away from me, I developed a pit of hatred for the man. I even went so far as to think he had a crush on her, but the way he looked at Tessa was never quite right enough to make that fit. Most of the time he looked at her the way Gary always did, like she was his child and he wanted to protect her. I never could fault him for that and Chief does still look at her the same way, but she doesn't need his protection. She has mine.

I yank a pill from Dr. Lafferty's satchel and crunch it between my teeth. Tessa's been doing her dang best to stay off of me but Marcie is the opposite, and now I'm glad Tessa has been blocking my advances. The next time I think I'm in bad shape I'll remember it can always be worse.

"Tessa!" I shout, dragging my unwilling body out of the bedroom and down the hall. Words are still coming out of Marcie's mouth but I've heard all I need to hear. The click of that front door wasn't just Chief leaving, it's Tessa.

I stomp through the living room. Marcie yanks my arm, doing little to keep me away from the front door. "Let her go, Warren. Chief said I can take you out of this town. We're getting out of Hinton for good. We're going to have those kids you said you wanted."

I shove her away from me and throw the door open, stomping over the porch with a rattle in my chest that makes my whole body shake. Chief's car is on its way down the gravel drive. "Tessa!" Her name rips from my throat. Chief's car keeps moving. I jump off the porch and let out a yell, the pain slicing through my body only increasing my rage. The bastard isn't even tapping his brakes. He's stealing what's mine and despite her promises, Tessa is letting him. Because this is what she's had in her head the whole time. She's going after Beth on her own.

I push into a sprint. Pain explodes through my lungs. I hit my knees, gravel digging into the worn fabric of my pants. I cough up blood and choke on what feels like part of my throat, my knuckles sprayed red as my palms press into the rock. I lean forward, blurry eyes fixed on Chief's fading taillights. Marcie's hands wrap over my shoulders, frantic and tugging, trying to lift me from the ground. "Stop this foolishness! You can barely stand. If Tessa cared about that she'd be here, but she's not. She's gone! Let her go. It's what she wants."

Marcie leaves off trying to get me up and wraps her arms around my neck. "*I'm* here, and you love me too. I know you do. So please, Warren, don't go chasing after her again. All you ever get from chasing Tessa is hurt." Marcie loosens her arms and leans back, intercepting the track of my eyes, making her face all I can see. "Come back inside, rest, and then I'll drive us away from this place."

I lift a bloody hand and rake it through her hair, tugging her locks into my fist and pulling tight, something I've never done to Marcie before. "Tessa leaving here tonight is your fault, and so is everything that happens to her from here on out. So get the hell off of me." I shove her head free of my grip. She scrambles backward over the grass, fear thick in those eyes that I've tried to lose myself in time and again. But the difference between Marcie and Tessa is as obvious as the difference between a toad and a tiger. Right now, I wish Tessa was more like Marcie, minus the sobbing. Marcie's tears are only stoking my anger.

I push off the ground and stumble back to the porch, smashing the flower pots lining the side to keep from laying hands on Marcie again. Deep down I know this really isn't her fault, but I can't see straight right now, let alone think straight.

I throw the door open and swipe an arm over the table where Chief's keys should be, breaking the ceramics and throwing a vase through the lamp on the other side of the living room. It's not Chief's family's fault either, but when you lay with pigs you're bound to get their filth on you. I yank their family photo from the wall and smash it over the end of the table, continuing my reign of destruction all the way to the master bedroom, smashing the bedside lamps and toppling the dresser. Marcie squeals from the doorway behind me, the sound making me cringe. I snatch the satchel of pills from the bedside table and stuff them into the one pocket on the left side of my cargo pants that doesn't have a hole in it. Easy access, because I'm going to need all of these before this freaking night is over. Tessa might be dumb enough to think she can find Beth before the wolves find her, but she can't. Whether it's Hinton or Montrose's strays, they'll get her first.

I shove a hand under the pillow I've been using, yanking my knife free of the bed. I unsheathe it and stab it straight into the mattress, ripping the fabric and foam right down to the box springs. "What do you think, Marcie? Will Chief know I'm pissed?"

"I... You... He..." she stammers, nearly drowning on her sobs.

My heart sinks. Marcie coming here *is* the reason Tessa left but it was Chief using Marcie that took Tessa away from me. Something he wouldn't have been able to do if I'd gotten in front of this situation. I knew Marcie would be worried sick about me. I should have sent Tessa out with a message for her, but I was too worried sick about Tessa becoming dead, or worse, to spare much time caring about anyone else's feelings.

I put my knife away, securing it to me, and walk toward Marcie with more restraint than I feel capable of having right now. "Marcie, I tried to keep you out of this but you didn't stay out, so now you're going to have to grow some thick skin real quick because things only get worse from here. Now, did you bring a phone with you?"

She nods, tears sprinkling out of her eyes as she points toward the purse she dropped by the foot of the bed. I yank it off the floor and dump the contents onto the wrecked bed, grinding my teeth together when Marcie yelps. "Noises like that are the exact opposite of having thick skin, Marcie."

She snatches the phone out of the rubble and shoves it into my chest. "Well what do you expect when you're yelling and screaming at me, Warren? *I'm* the one who's here for you. I've *been* here for you while Tessa treats you like dirt. But you don't care." Tears slide from her eyes and her voice hitches. "You said you loved me."

I take the phone from her shaking hand, clocking the tremor in her shoulders at the touch of my fingers on hers. She's scared of me now. Good. "Every time I said I loved you, you told me I was lying. I guess you were right."

I dial Jimmy, savoring the dull relief of the pain pills and considering if I should go ahead and take a handful or just snort the stuff. "It's me."

"About time," he snarls. "Marcie's mom ambushed me with a *kiss*, while she was *naked*, and tried to get me into bed. And apparently all so your girlfriend could sneak off. Do you know what it's like to have an old woman's tongue in your mouth?"

I pace away from Marcie, moving to the window and pulling the blind back, shouldering the frame and scanning the yard. "Shut up, Jimmy. Listen to me. I'm at Chief's place and I'm not in the best of shape. I need you to me bring the biggest freaking gun you have and a truckload of ammo. Got it?"

He groans. "Since you're not dead yet, yeah, I got it. But you better start paying me some of what you owe me because it sounds like you're still running around trying to get yourself killed."

My jaw ticks. I drop the blind. "If I do die, you can have Town's End. But the club rightfully owns it so you'll be working for them and I doubt repaying my loan will get you out of that so bring me some weapons and take back this woman you lost while making out with her mother."

I hang up on him and hobble toward the door. Marcie stands in front of me, arms folding over her chest in an attempt to look like she's growing a backbone. "You forgot to tell him that we're all going to die because of your stupid ex."

I reach out, her flinch calling her bluff. I wrap my fingers around her forearm, yanking her limbs free and lifting her palm. I drop her phone into it. "And you forgot to stay where I told you to stay, so I guess we're even. Now pull yourself together because if we don't die, it'll be because my dumbass ex is out there doing her best to save us."

Her face falls. "You're never going to pick me over her, are you? Never."

A pang of guilt sharpens its teeth on my heart. "According to you, we're all going to die, so no, I guess not."

Her head dips, tears falling in thick sheets. I curse myself for making that happen. "Look at me, Marcie." She does, eyes red and watery. "I do love you. A lot. That's why I left you with Jimmy. You were safe with him, because everyone knows I love Tessa a hell of a lot more than anyone else. So don't torture yourself by making me say it to your face because I don't have time to coddle you right now. Tessa is out there and we have more enemies than we have friends. So learn something from this. When I send you away with Jimmy this time, stay gone."

~||~

Tessa

Warren's shout won't leave my ears. No matter how far away from Chief's house I go, I can still hear Warren, see his form falling to the ground in the glow of the taillights. Of all the many things I've done to him, this is right up there with the worst of them. Another thing for me to be ashamed over. I wasted so many of the years we had together, ignored what he sensed in Beth all along, and let him down time and again. He won't see what I'm doing now as anything other than another betrayal, but in spite of how despicable I am, Warren loves me. So while his loyal Marcie is around to slow him down, I'll tend to the mess I made of our lives, our club, and our town.

Chief turns onto Main Street. "You're doing the right thing, Tessa."

My mouth runs dry, all the way down my throat and into the darkest parts of me. "Don't give me credit for being what I've already proved I'm not. We all know Marcie is the better woman but I'm not going to let Warren have her." I turn from the window and stare at the ticking vein in Chief's neck, the echo of Warren's voice in my head overpowering the resolve I thought I had. I don't want to be away from him any more than he wants me gone. "There was a time when I would have clocked a girl for staring at Warren for too long. Those days are here again. When I'm finished setting Hinton back to rights, I'm going set Warren and me back together. Marcie can let go of him willingly or we can fight for him, either way, Warren is mine."

Chief's fingers tighten around the steering wheel. "*I'll* be the one to set Hinton back to rights and you're not going to touch a hair on that girl's head. She's been through enough. Heck, half her family is dead because..."

"Because of me." I finish what he left off saying. "Her aunt and sister are dead because Beth needed targets that would get Warren away from me. But it didn't work and that blood is on my hands so believe me when I say I'm ashamed that I'm the reason for all of Marcie's pain. She only gets what I give her though, and her days with Warren are numbered."

Chief's eyes dart across the seats. "You beat that girl down and I'll bury you under my jail, you hear me?"

I snort. "If I don't survive, you can have the honor of burying me. Then you can let Marcie know that she only gets Warren in this life so she better make it a good one because I'll be waiting for him on the other side. I don't care how many years she has with him or how many babies they have together, he's mine, not hers. I'll wait on him forever knowing that."

I already tried to talk my heart into not belonging to Warren but it didn't listen. All it did was stop talking to me, and that got me into a whole heap of trouble that spilled over into the lives of every other citizen in Hinton. "Falling on your sword is for idiots, Chief, so that's not what I'm doing. I'm keeping Warren out of as much of this mess as I can, but he's going to come for me, and he'll find me. So get us someplace safe. We need a plan and we need it quick."

~

Chief pulls into the small concrete driveway in front of Erin's house. The place isn't large but it's nicer than mine, with a level yard that's fenced in and shaded, her son's toys strewn about and a swing set off to the side. "Are you sure this is where you want to be?" I ask Chief.

He sighs. "It gets you out of Hinton. I'll send Erin and the boy off on a little vacation."

I open my door. "Send them to where you sent your wife. I'm sure they'll all be safer together."

"Very funny," he huffs, opening his own door and getting out. He walks around the front of the vehicle. "Erin's car isn't here. She's not working so she should be home but I just gave her money to put new tires on her car so maybe she's off doing that." He hands me a key. "Go on inside. I'm going to call Erin and let her know I'm here, and see if I can hurry her along so she can come home and pack."

I take the key and walk toward the front door, scanning the toys in the yard as I go, longing pulling at me from all directions. I want this life with Warren. A house of our own, a yard full of kids' toys to trip over on my way to the grill, and maybe even a dog or two.

I slide the key into the slot and open the door, stepping into the small living room and closing the door behind me. The house is silent but it doesn't feel empty. "Erin?" I call out. Her car isn't here but it could be in the shop, or borrowed. "It's Tessa. Chief gave me a key."

No one responds. I move past the checkered couch and step over a coloring book splayed on the floor between the living room and kitchen. A smell hits my nose, something familiar hanging in the air. I can't quite place it but my worn nerves are on edge, body tense as I move farther into the kitchen, rounding the corner and passing the silver refrigerator that's sticking out. My foot slides. I look down. The creamy tile is puddled with dark liquid. I follow the trail, setting my eyes on the overturned chair, the body seeping blood beside it reminding me of what the smell is. Copper.

I drop down beside Erin, checking for a pulse though I already know there isn't one. Beth's been here. She's the only person sick enough to carve Erin's face up like this, the edges of her mouth now reaching all the way to her ears. Her shirt is in place but I don't look under the bloody top. I've seen Beth's handiwork enough to know what the slab of flesh falling out of that shirt means. I rest my hand over Erin's eyes and pull them closed. She's cold, but not so much that this murder happened days ago. Beth killed Erin recently. Erin who has a child.

"Caleb?" I call the boy's name, climbing off the floor next to his mother. There's a tiny thump against the wall. I race back around the corner, my hand instinctively going for the nearest weapon. I doubt Beth is still here, she'll be the reason Erin's car is missing, but in case I'm wrong, I'll not meet her unarmed. I slide the butcher knife from the block and keep racing for the hallway. "Caleb?"

The first door is a bathroom. Of the two across from each other at the end of the hall, one is open and the other closed. I scan Erin's room before throwing open her son's door. Arnold is beside the racecar bed. Naked. One scrawny leg stuffed into a pair of jeans. My head goes fuzzy, inky blackness working its way forward as anger vibrates through my skull. Behind Arnold, on the bed, is Caleb, his naked body red and swollen, face frozen in a scream surely meant for his mother. One stifled by the plastic bag covering his head.

My grip on the knife tightens, Chopper's lessons rising up. He taught me how to properly hold a blade when you want your stab to count. I stare into the terror of Caleb's lifeless eyes and want this to count double. I lunge at Arnold, elbow cocked tighter than a bowstring. I aim for his heart. He throws up an arm, blocking my blade but not my body. We collide. His foot tangles in his half-on pair of pants, tripping him. I land on top of him, cocking the knife and bringing it down again, this time aiming for the space where the neck meets the shoulder. He bucks. My blade glances off his collarbone.

"I didn't mean to!" he shouts, bucking again and smashing his fist into my face.

I canter sideways, my knife looking for purchase anywhere it can find it. I clip his arm. He punches me in the side of the face, sending my head careening into the corner of the bed frame. Light flashes behind my lids. I swing back around, met by Arnold's fist. It makes contact with my nose and I swing out wildly. He scrambles backward, getting his feet under him and shoving his other leg into the pants as he stands. I launch off the floor but this time, he's ready. His body turns, his elbow swinging around and connecting with my jaw. I swipe my blade across his stomach, opening a bloody gash above the body part I intend to cut off. He yells. I don't hesitate. I drop my shoulder and pounce, crashing into his chest and bowling him over. He hits the floor, air whooshing out of him. I cock the knife and slam it through the soft flesh in his side, just below his ribs. He shouts, clocking me in the jaw. My head snaps to the side and Arnold rolls, scrabbling away from me.

"Tessa?" Chief's yell rings through the house.

Arnold freezes. I drop down beside him and yank the knife back out, relishing in the fact that this blade cuts both ways. "Here, Chief!"

Arnold's survival instinct kicks back in and he throws an elbow into my face. I plant my knife into his gut. He clocks my other jaw. Blood bursts in my mouth. I spit it on him, all the fight draining from his limbs as Chief stumbles into the room, a sound rattling out of Chief's throat, one of a pain that can't be cured. Of a sorrow only borne one way. Arnold has to die, and as he watches Chief rip the bag from his son's head, Arnold's eyes tell me he knows it. They're full of a different kind of sorrow as he watches the father cradle the boy in his arms, rocking his son's lifeless body with tears rushing down his face and anger cutting off all the words he's trying to shout.

I wrap both my hands around the knife, staring into Arnold's defeated eyes as I twist the blade. Before I take his life for what he did to that boy, I want answers. "Where. Is. Beth?"

A sob breaks from his throat. "I don't know."

I rip the blade out of him, his blood coating my hands. "Liar."

"I swear!" His mouth flaps like a dying fish, slobber stringing across his lips as he sputters. "I don't know where she is. She's crazy. And she..." His eyes dart to Chief.

I kneel on Arnold's chest, pressing the tip of my blade into the small of his neck. "You haven't seen crazy yet, but you're about to."

He sucks in air, my full weight making it hard for him to take the next breath. "I didn't touch Erin. That was all Beth. And she told me to take the boy. To play the game with him that she lets me play with the other kids. I just did what she said."

Vomit rushes up my throat. I lever the blade up, pressing the tip down into his skin, my face leaning to within an inch of his. "You put a bag over his head, you sick bastard."

Snot runs down Arnold's face. "I didn't. I only did what I always do. What the kids like. Then Beth came with the bag and she said he'd like it more that way. And he did," Arnold blubbers. "Caleb did. I watched his face and he lik—"

A piece of Arnold's skull sticks into my chin. I lift my shaking blade from the neck that no longer has a head, an oozing ball of red all that's left in front of me. I get off his chest and wipe the bits of Arnold away from my eyes, smearing the blood from my hands to what's coating my face, everything in slow motion as I straighten my body from where the barrel of Chief's gun is still smoking. He drew so fast I never saw him move. I blink, lashes sticking together. Through the coated haze, I meet Chief's eyes. He issues one order. "Bring me your sister."

~12~

My ears ring, shock slowing the blood in my veins while forcing thoughts to race through my mind. I stare at Chief, his gun, his son… I hear the crack of the door, the shattering of glass, the explosion of boots over hardwood floors… None of it puts motion back into my limbs. I can't move. My heart wants me to reach out to Chief, to console an inconsolable man. One whose life will never be the same again. My head wants me to yell at him. We needed information from Arnold.

A howl clatters out of Chief, the kind of bellow that peels the skin from your bones. My hands itch, slick with sweat and blood, and I run them over my pants as he hits the floor, scrabbling to the side of his son's bed. The little boy's body, slick and red with its own blood, is shimmering with glass from the broken window that shot across it. Rough hands grab me from behind, Randy's shout in my ear too loud and Zeno's throwing knife too accurate. Chief's gun is on the floor beside his bleeding arm. "Stop." I push the sound through numb lips, the force of Randy's pull dragging me from the little boy's bedroom. "Stop!" I flail my arms wide, grab for the doorframe, the wall, anything I can find purchase on. Randy jerks me harder. My body smacks the wall, my head clipping the bathroom door. Randy shoves me inside and spins away just as fast as he grabbed me.

I whip around. Shaun steps into the doorframe, arms folded over his chest and hard eyes digging into me. "Chief," I swallow. "His son…"

"We saw," Shaun answers. "That's why he's not dead. Shower. Now."

I stare into his eyes, finding no trace of the friendship we once shared. I walk toward him, no intention of trying to get past his blockade. I just want to look at him. "I'm glad you're not dead. You, Randy, and Zeno. Who else is left?" He doesn't answer. Doesn't move. Not a tick of a jaw or a softening of his eyes. I turn away from him and step into the tub, pulling the shower curtain closed. "I watched Chopper's head get blown off and I held Gary's guts in my hands so believe me, Shaun, seeing all of you alive and breathing is worth being covered in brains for."

His silence is all that answers me. I turn on the water and let it wash over me, not bothering to remove my clothes. They have more of Arnold on them than my skin does. I turn my face into the stream and scrub, wishing I could wash away the images behind my eyelids. Beth might not have intended for me to find Erin and Caleb, but she knew I'd hear about it. These murders were a message. To me, and to anyone who's even thinking about helping me. It didn't take a genius to see Erin's kid and not know who the father was, so out of town or not, people will connect these dots and they'll understand the language Beth is using. No one is safe from her wrath. Not even the chief of police.

I turn off the water, the last bits of Arnold swirling down the drain. "Out. Change." Shaun's voice filters through the curtain. I slide it open. There's jeans and a t-shirt folded on the sink. Shaun shoves a towel at me.

I take it and he raises his eyes over my head, keeping them open. He isn't going to turn away. This is all the privacy I'm getting.

I strip off my wet clothes and run the towel over my body. I doubt Shaun will sneak more of a peek than what his eyes can already see from their current perch but even if he did, I'm finding it hard to care. He was there when Chopper found the pictures Beth and Matt took of me. Plus, he's the heartthrob of Hinton. Women young and old are at his disposal and I'm certain my body holds no fascination for him. Warren is the only one who would be mad about this situation and I have no doubt he's on his way to finding me right now. I don't want to be with the club when he does.

I tug the t-shirt over my head. Judging from the size and the fact that we're in Erin's house, these clothes are hers. I smooth my fingers over the fabric, blood cold as ice. These are the remnants of yet another life that I destroyed. If Beth didn't hate me so much, Erin would be alive. Her son. And the ripple of their deaths wouldn't have destroyed Chief.

I button the jeans and Shaun steps aside, letting me pass through the doorway. He motions to Erin's bedroom, where Randy's wide shoulders are visible. I step into the doorframe. Chief has a thick bandage on his wrist and a child cradled to his chest. Randy and I watch silently as Chief tucks his son into Erin's arms. I look up at Randy. I don't know which one of them carried Erin to her bed, but after Gary and Chopper, Randy is next in line to lead the Hinton Charter so this didn't happen without his blessing, and Erin didn't deserve to be left on the cold floor any more than that boy deserved to be left in his room alone. "Thank you."

Randy doesn't respond. He's not even looking at me. He turns to the door and moves out of the room, giving Chief the privacy I haven't been afforded. I follow Randy. He expects it, and if I don't do even the things he's not vocalizing, he won't hesitate to make me.

He stops in the living room and I fall in line at his side, scanning the Leidolf gathered in the small space. Zeno and Shaun are here, along with Brian and even one of Montrose's former men. Carl won't make eye contact with me any more than the others will. Shaun is the only one who meets my eye and his stare is anything but friendly.

I look down at the frayed edges of the jeans. I suppose I don't deserve anything more from the club but once the shock of having a man's head explode an inch from my face wears off, I imagine I'm not going to care as much about what I deserve. I want to celebrate with them, happy they're all alive. I also want to run from them, find Warren and hide him away from men whose intentions I can no longer claim to know.

"The sister is just the beginning of the rot in Hinton," Randy speaks, easing the rapid build of the tension. "Tessa will make us a list of all the kids Beth babysat for and we'll find out who is like Arnold. They'll share his fate."

The others make a ratifying sound. Chief walks into the small room, crowding in with the rest of us. "You bring me the names of any man or woman responsible for hurting children and I'll see to it that they're eradicated. But I also want Beth. I want to know why she came all the way here just to hurt Erin and our boy."

I bite back a curse. Erin moved out of town to hide Chief's secret but the only thing Beth didn't know was how much Chief truly loved Erin. I saw the couple together and didn't even realize how deep or genuine their feelings were until recently. "Beth did this because she wants me alone and isolated, and must have somehow known that I was with you, Chief."

The weight of my confession draws more tension into the room. Because I called Chief for help, his family died. "Beth wants me all to herself. Always has."

Randy's arm adjusts, his hand gripping my upper arm. "She's too late. We already called dibs." He looks at what are now his men. "Let's move."

"Wait." I put up as much resistance as I dare. "Beth is getting away with the things she's doing because she's dragging other people into it, finding all the sick ones and exploiting them for her own gain. I can put a stop to it. Beth is doing this to get to me, so give *me* to her. Let me go and don't follow me. I'll find her or she'll find me. Either way, I'll kill her. Then I'll come back to the club and face whatever I have to." I shift, begging Randy to look at me. "I swear it. I'll come back to you."

~

Warren

I stand guard on Chief's porch, watching the darkness for signs of Jimmy. It's hot out. Sweat beads across my back and runs down my spine, dipping underneath the band of my cargo pants and doing nothing to warm the chill running through my veins. Tessa is scrappier than most but that doesn't make me feel any better about her being out there alone facing who knows what. Chief might be of help where Beth is concerned but he won't measure up to the wolves. Not the Leidolf or a single one of Montrose's strays. They'll put a bullet in him before he even knows they're there. If he tries to take Beth alive, so will Tessa, because breath being left in Beth's body is the one thing Tessa will never allow. When she sets eyes on Beth, Tessa isn't going to stop until her sister is gone from this world and she's not going to care if she gets herself killed in the process. Because Tessa's a freaking martyr and all Chief has done since bringing us here is feed her complex.

I take another pill out of my pocket and chew it up. If Chief had a lick of sense he'd see that Tessa and I have barely been staying half a step ahead of our pursuers, found every place we go, and that he just stacked the deck against us both all because he's petty. He might not care if I die but he'll care if she does. And if she does, I'll make sure I live long enough to make him regret the choices he made today.

"You shouldn't worry about her so much." Marcie's cold voice slithers over my shoulder. "Tessa's like gum on the bottom of your shoe. Always sticking around and ruining what everyone else has worked for."

I take my time scanning the yard, regretting more than ever having gotten myself into this relationship with Marcie. I face her. "You're right, Tessa is one heck of a good luck charm. But not even she can outrun what's coming for us all. And I thought I told you to stay in the bedroom?"

Her chin lifts. "You want my skin thick? This is it. Tessa doing the opposite of everything you say turns you on, so now it's my turn."

I march to the patch of porch her feet are glued to and wrap my hand around her arm. "You're picking a fine time to grow a pair but unlike when Tessa loses her cool, all you're managing to do is piss me off." I bite down and yank her back into the house, doing my best to throw her onto the couch with a gentle hand. "Plant yourself into those cushions deep enough that you sprout roots."

She springs upright, crawling backward on the couch like a cat who's getting ready to run out of its skin. "Don't you see what Tessa's done to you? What she's turned you into? You're abusing me and you have Jimmy coming here with guns so you can go after the chief of Hinton's police department!"

I swipe a palm over my forehead to dry the sweat. "The way I see it, Chief turned me into this. But don't you worry, if he's as lucky as Tessa is, he'll be able to talk around the barrel I'm getting ready to shove down his throat."

She slides her back down the couch, knees tucked into her chest. "You're worse than the drunk everyone always said you'd be. You're under the influence of *her* and treating the rest of us like you don't care if we live or die!"

The vein in my neck ticks. I count the pulses, doing my best to calm down. "Marcie, caring about whether or not you die is exactly why I put you with Jimmy. He's a one-man army with that gun of his. If he can see it, he can shoot it."

"Then why don't you put him with your precious Tessa?" she seethes.

I shake my head at her. "If I put Jimmy on Tessa, then Jimmy would be in the thick of things because *Tessa* is the heart of all this. Not by her own doing but by the doings of people who want to use her. So like *you*, Jimmy never had to be part of this and wouldn't have been if it wasn't for our moron of a police chief." I lean into her face. "I'm not the type of man to haul off and hit a woman, but you're real close to having me bust you in the mouth. The last time I had an urge to strike a female like this, it was Beth, and I wish now that I would have let that fury inside of me unleash because I'd rather be sitting in prison for beating a woman to death than standing here listening to you snivel because you're jealous of a woman who's out there sacrificing herself for everyone in this whole town."

Marcie's body stills. "Sacrificing? What do you think I've been doing? My aunt and sister are dead because of her. Because *you* refuse to let go of her. And then I'm forced to sit under lock and key because a bunch of bikers you're only associated with because of Tessa want to kidnap me to get to you. And she's the person you think is sacrificing?"

I straighten. "If the club thought picking you up would draw me out, they would have done it already. But everyone left you alone because you're a well-known waste of their time."

Tears slide from her eyes. "I stayed in Hinton for you, worrying and praying. Tessa wouldn't even stay in this house for you. She left, not caring at all that you were screaming and writhing in pain."

Her words cut and tear, righter than they are wrong, but they don't carry half the weight of the misery I'll feel if Tessa dies tonight. "Sorry to disappoint you, sweetheart, but I've been forced to choose and I made my choice."

~13~

Marcie might have stayed in Hinton for me but Tessa stayed for everyone. Long before I convinced Gary to put me on Tessa's hide, he sent her off with Chopper. She didn't stay gone. Despite her hard exterior, for the people she loves and even those she doesn't really like, she'll put herself out. And Beth knows Tessa as well as I do. That's why Beth's manipulation is full of mind games that use Tessa's own heart against her. It was Beth who planted seeds of doubt about me into Tessa's head, fueling and spurring others on to have the same opinion of me until those seeds were well watered. They sprouted when Tessa's self-esteem was at an all-time low. A time when my own was dwindling. Tessa ran from me then, same as she's doing now. Only this time it's because she thinks running will save me. It might, but it's not going to save her.

I meet Jimmy at Chief's front door. "It's about time."

He hands me a rifle, a matching one slung over his shoulder. "You called me less than half an hour ago and in case you didn't know, there's still a curfew in effect and law is crawling all over this town. I had to drive the old logging roads just to get out here."

I take the rifle and check the chamber. "Is this all you brought?"

He throws his hands up. "What did you want me to bring you? I'm a deer hunter, Warren. I don't have grenade launchers lying around."

He might not, but the club does. I've seen their arsenal. Shaun goes out of his way to deal in the heavy stuff. He likes his weapons big, loud, and destructive. "I have a cache at Town's End, if Chief Piggy didn't find it. Have you heard anything about the garage or the club?"

His eyes narrow. "I've been a little busy doing your babysitting."

Marcie's mom runs across the porch, shoving Jimmy into the barrel of the rifle I'm holding on her way through the door. I hit him with it again. "Did I tell you to bring her with you?"

He jams a finger in his ear as the woman screeches. "What was I supposed to do with her? You told me to watch her and I told her to wait in the truck." He shoves his hand in the direction of the wailing both Marcie and her mom are now doing. "And you dragging me into this, cousin? Whatever you're paying me just tripled."

"Money?" Marcie's mom shouts. "How are you thinking about a thing like that? Just look at what these monsters are doing to my daughter. They already got one killed and now they're torturing my poor Marcie!"

I shoulder the rifle I'm grateful to have and drag a hand down my face, walking back into the room where Marcie is huddled in the corner crying her eyes out. Her mom is a pile of sobs right beside her. "Mavis, if you want to blame someone for what your daughter is going through right now, blame Chief. It was his choice to bring her here, just like it was *your* choice to ambush Jimmy so she could."

"No!" Marcie screams. "This is all Tessa's fault. She's a devil. Just like her sister!"

"Her sister?" Jimmy questions. "I know Tessa's got a mean streak a mile long but what's Beth ever done to anyone?"

I've not cared much about Chief's reluctance to name Beth in the murders. Putting her on blast would only make her scurry deeper into hiding, tipping her off that we were all coming for her. Tessa, me, the law, and every true wolf left alive. But not shouting her name from the rooftops leads to another unsuspecting person losing their life. People trust Beth, if for no other reason than her being Tessa's sister. Beth has lived her life cashing in on that card. "Beth likes to cut people up, Jimmy. She likes to slit the throats of little girls and rip out the hearts of others because she's as jealous of Tessa as Marcie is. So I'm going to need you to get Marcie and her mouth out of here before she says or does something I'm going to have to make her regret."

Jimmy shoves me toward the kitchen. I groan, turning in the direction he's wanting because I can barely hold up my own weight. I don't need to deal with fighting his right now. I hobble to the counter and use it to take some of the pressure off my lungs. "What?"

His arms fold over his chest, that usually calm demeanor of his gone. "For starters, where am I supposed to take Marcie? I've been trying to get those crazy women in there to leave Hinton but they won't go. I even talked to Katherine up in Huntington and she has a place all ready for us. Teresa's body is being sent to her so we can do the service and all up there, but Marcie won't go because she's worried about you dying in bar shootouts!"

I fidget with the pills in my pocket, wanting more and knowing I shouldn't. "Katherine is a good plan, Jimmy. Whether Marcie wants to go to her older sister's place or not, go ahead and take her to Huntington. Stay there with them. Don't come back to Hinton unless I send for you."

"And if you don't send for us?" He does his best to whisper, the anger rolling off him making it more of a shout. "We were supposed to be changing our lives, living a dream you were building that would better our family for generations and now you're throwing it all away over a piece of tail you already had a thousand times over!"

I push off the counter, using the extra leverage to carry my fist into the side of his mouth. He stumbles backward, a trickle of blood seeping from his lower lip. My chest heaves. "You got one thing right. *I'm* building this. You can ride my coattails but I've heard enough of Tessa's name being run through the mud. If you want someone to talk about, flap your jaw about Beth, not Tessa, because *Beth* is the reason this dynasty fell apart. She's sick in the head and I'm going to relieve her of that sickness."

Jimmy wipes the blood off his mouth. "You can hit me all you want but it won't change the fact that you're in the middle of stuff you shouldn't be in, cousin. Stuff you wouldn't be anywhere near if it weren't for Tessa."

"You and those two women in there are the ones in the middle of something you don't belong in, and you're only wedged in it now because of *Chief* and his bad decisions. Ones he won't live to make again because I'm going to find him, and then I'm going to beat him to death for touching what's mine."

The color drains out of Jimmy's face. "You're serious. You're freaking serious?"

I nod. Ever since being faced with threats to Tessa's actual life, death has taken on a lighter meaning. I don't regret any of the killings I've done. Given the choice, I'd do it all over again. And after what I've seen recently, Chief is a danger to Tessa. He isn't giving in to her whims or being manipulated by her. He has an agenda and he's using her to get to what he wants. I don't have to know what he thinks he can get out of her, his end game is power, just like all the others, and Tessa is a bargaining chip. "Beth is going to die. Chief is going to die. And while I'm at it, I'm wolf hunting."

Jimmy runs both his hands up his face and through his hair, digging his fingers down the back of his head. "I don't understand you and I don't want to know what all is going on, I just thought you were looking for that easy life. A hard day's work, money in the bank, cold beer and a warm woman at night. All the things you have. Or had." He drops his hands. "I just want you to be okay and if you can't do that here, then come with us."

I squint against his sudden turn of emotion, his anger being swallowed up by sorrow. Tessa and I only survived this long because of the disruption Montrose's men caused. I wanted to use that to get her out of Hinton but I couldn't. "Nothing is okay anywhere, Jimmy. There's no place I can run, nowhere to hide. I'm as tied to the death and destruction in Hinton as Tessa is. And I'll either set it right again or I'll die trying. Which is what Tessa is trying to do even though she's going about it like she's dumber than a puppet on a string. So cut her some slack and stay off of my back. You've got the easy job. Get those women in there and go live the sweet life."

He presses his fingers to his brow, a mocking salute before turning away. "Let's go, ladies."

I walk into the living room behind him. Marcie and her mom are clutching each other like they're the ones getting ready to meet the fate I'm bound to give Chief. Jimmy waves a hand at them. "Get a move on. Moonlight is burning."

They scurry to the door and run out to his truck. We follow. He stops by his driver's door, staring at me. The look in his eyes might be right. This might be the last time we see each other. I give him a nod. "Drive that truck like you stole it and it's hotter than the tail end of a rattlesnake. Get these women out of Hinton and do what you've got to do. For yourself and for our family. Got it?"

He slings his rifle into the rack behind his seat. "Yeah, I got it. Just try not to get killed because I'd rather ride your coattails than build anything myself." He jumps into his seat. "Reporters are still parked across from Riverside Grille, turning one whole side of the street into a campground. Safety in numbers, I suppose. That, and the hope they'll catch the Leidolf sneaking back into their clubhouse."

I throw open the driver's door of the sedan Marcie came here in. "Thanks. I'll get in touch with you when I can."

He slams his truck door, his engine roaring to life and blocking out what I know we're both thinking. I'll call him *if* I survive. And he's too attached to his money to bet on me living through this.

"Warren!" Marcie bails from his truck and races to my door.

I rest my rifle in the floorboard of the passenger seat. "We don't have time for this, Marcie. Get in Jimmy's truck."

"I will," she cries, looking at me the same way Jimmy did. Like it's the last time she'll ever see me.

I mutter a string of curses that would make mine and Jimmy's grandma hit us over the head with her skillet if she ever heard such words, getting out of the car and gripping Marcie's shoulders. "You're the sweetest person I know and I don't want to be mean to you, but I can't have you in the middle of this. So stop doing the opposite of everything I tell you to do or I'm going to end up hurting you. And I'm not talking about hurting your feelings with my words. I'm talking pain, Marcie. So get your backside in Jimmy's truck and do every freaking thing he tells you to do from this minute forward."

She nods. "I am. I just need you to know that I love you. That I still love you and I'm scared. Please come with us."

I turn her loose. "I can't."

"Because of *her*?" She sniffs, flicking syllables off her tongue like even referring to Tessa coats her tongue in tar. "Do I mean anything at all to you?"

I point at Jimmy's truck. "My feelings might not be good enough for you but I have them. You mean a lot to me, Marcie. But Tessa means a hell of a lot more. Now go."

Tears shake loose from her eyes. "There's only one of us you're sending away. Let that sink in for you, Warren. *I'm* the one you're protecting the most. So I'll just have to keep praying that Tessa's miserable life ends with that horrible death I've been praying she'll die."

"Darn it, Marcie!" I yank her away from the car and drag her back to Jimmy's truck, my grip sure to leave a bruising reminder on her arm. "You can say whatever messed up crap you want to say to me, but don't take your hurt feelings out on Tessa. You know where my loyalty lies. So be mad at me, set all my things on fire, sleep with random men on the riverbank, or do whatever else makes you feel like you're really letting me have it. Just keep Tessa's name out of your mouth." I pick Marcie up and throw her onto the seat, glaring at Jimmy. "How many times do I have to tell you to get her out of here?"

He flips me off. I slam the truck door, turning toward the sedan. Marcie's keys hit me in the back of the head. I spin around and glare at her. She rolls the window back up, still having the nerve to yell one last barb. "I love you more than she does!"

I rip the keys I don't need off the ground. I know how to hotwire a car and I had one like hers at Town's End. It came to me by questionable means and I put the ignition back together myself. The woman who brought it to me was married to a man who got a twenty-year-old girl pregnant, his actions being her reward for staying hitched to him for twenty-five years. I figured I should just buy the car and not question the state it was in.

I get into the sedan and start it up. Jimmy's taillights are already fading out of sight. I shift into gear. Marcie might love me more than Tessa does, and Tessa's stupid nine times out of ten. But I'm crazy about her eleven out of seven. She's the only woman who irritates me from sunup to sundown, and I don't want anyone but her.

~14~

I grip the steering wheel with both hands and make a hard right, hitting an old logging road. All these bygone trails interconnect and weave through most of the wooded acreage in Hinton, but few of these roads are fit for vehicles and this is one that isn't. Deep ruts cut down either side of it and there are holes in between those. I hit every one of them none too easy. Two cop cars fly past me, down the road I just turned off of, lights and sirens shouting. A horrible feeling creeps up my gut. Those cars are on their way to Chief's house. He sent them to find me, and that means he's already breaking from the deals he made with Tessa. I never trusted him and now I know that she can't.

Despite everything, Tessa's under my skin in a way that can't ever be undone and I know for a fact that I'm stuck in her bone-deep. She'd die for me and I'd gladly give my life for hers, but I'm not trying to. So I hope the only threat out here tonight is Beth because taking on a pack of rabid wolves with only my knife and Jimmy's spare hunting rifle is a death sentence and I already came close enough to dying. The only thing worse would be me having to bury Tessa. I won't do it. And if something happens to me, she has no place left to turn. Especially if the Leidolf won't eat the crow I intend to force down their throats.

I press my foot against the gas pedal and yank the wheel left, knowing all of these overgrown, rutted-out roads almost as well as I know the lines of Tessa's face. My head bangs off the roof lining, sending a jolt of pain through me with each hit of a hole I don't bother trying to miss. I'm working on a high to make the sky jealous, but even with dulled senses, my plan isn't a good one. In this condition, I'm likely to lose a fight with a wet paper bag. But I'm out of time and I never had many options to begin with. I need to find a wolf den before it finds Tessa.

I skid the sedan to a stop two hundred yards from the main road. With curfew still in effect and my garage being this far out of town, there isn't any news activity. I get out of the car and race through the woods, branches slicing at my face as I cut a stumbling path out to the pavement. I stop near the edge, just before the hardtop, and hunker down. Town's End is across the road. There are a few lights scattered around the property, solar flood lamps that I installed to keep the front parking lot lit up. Other lights are set for motion detection and none of those are on. The club could have disabled them, or the wolves could just be sitting so perfectly still that nothing is being triggered.

I dip a hand into my pocket and pull out two more pills, crunching and holding them under my tongue so the medicine jumps straight into action. If this is the time when I pay my final respects to the club, so be it. Just so long as they let me pay Tessa's too. My brothers have more than a little explaining to do. They were supposed to have this town on lockdown while looking out for Tessa. The Leidolf were the people who weren't supposed to be wearing blinders. The protectors. But they never had a bead on Beth because they never looked at her. They let her get away with killing just like they let Matt Honaker get to Tessa. Rick specifically. He was the one in charge of checking out the neighbors and he barely glanced at the jacked-up insurance salesman. So even if he does fall on his knees in front of Tessa, he doesn't get forgiveness.

I silently count to three and push into a run, heading straight for the back corner of the Snack Shack where the building blocks the light shining down on the open front end of the shed. I make it to the shadows and wonder if my vending machines are empty. It's surprising how much money these things rake in. Bobby Baker is the kind of man only his mother likes, but he stops by here on his way to work every day because I stock those little horn-shaped chips and he says he can't find them anywhere else. He's good for a bag of chips, a soda, and two candy bars. If my machines are empty, that's a chunk of cash I'm missing out on from just one customer. Not something I should be worried about at a time like this. A stupid grin lops onto my face. The appeal of these drugs is getting stronger by the minute.

I snort up a bloody loogie and spit it out, looking around, as hyper and alert as a man can be. I watch the moths circling the lights with one eye and keep the other on anything that dares to move out here tonight. Like those lightning bugs flashing across the street. They all catch my attention at once. I'm starting to feel like Superman. If I had Tommy's old bedsheet, I might climb to the top of this Snack Shack and see if I could fly across the lot instead of having to run again. But I'm fresh out of bedding and I need firepower. As risky as it is to be here and no matter how much it sucks to run, I won't know if all of my guns are gone until I check. Between Chief and the club I'm likely to leave here still only having this rifle that's slung over my shoulder.

The most likely cache to stay hidden is the one in the garage attached to my house. It's in the back of Tessa's Highlander, a false bottom on the box hiding my weapons. Even if someone opened the cache, unless they were interested in her clothes and cans of potted meat, they most likely left the box alone.

I take one last look around, draw a breath into my aching lungs, and set off on what's passing for a run. Jimmy's rifle beats against my back. I reach a hand back, steadying it, my nerves standing on end. Nothing is moving with me out here, but that doesn't mean I'm alone.

I reach the side of the garage and lean against the door, listening for any sound coming from inside. No racket except for the sound of my pounding heart. I punch the code into the door lock, Tessa's birthdate backward. The door clicks open and I move into the garage. The Highlander is right where I parked it after I stole it from Tessa. She got away from the club in it so I took her wheels because I've always been protective of her but ever since our split, my anger has sent me looking for trouble more often than not. My current plan is a prime example. If the club wants me dead, they'll manage to do the job, and me looking for them will make it easier. But I'll take some of them down with me and I'll do my best to convince the others to give Tessa the grace she mostly deserves.

I flip on the overhead light and trudge over to the Highlander, sliding the rifle off my shoulder and resting it against the side. I round the back and lift the hatch. A hand darts from underneath, clamping around my throat like a vice. I gag, voice cut off as Rick emerges from the dark inside of the vehicle. His body thrusts forward. My back slams into the workbench behind me. I send a fist into Rick's gut, thrashing left at the same time. His grip on my neck only tightens, fingers digging in, wrapping around my windpipe. I've been here before. Chopper did the same thing.

I throw my weight forward, running Rick back toward the Highlander. His side rams into the corner and he pivots, using the grip on my neck to sling me around, planting me into the side of the vehicle. "As soon as I found that box, I knew you'd come here, Gripr."

I throw another fist into his gut, shoving my other arm over his opposite shoulder. I wind that hand around the back of his head and bring him forward, smashing him face-first into the vehicle I'm glued to. His grip loosens. I stumble sideways, slinging a punch. "If I would have known you were here waiting for me, I would have come sooner. I owe you for letting the neighborhood pig have his way with Tessa."

Rick ducks under my fist, coming up elbow first, bringing the bone careening into my jaw. I wobble and he rushes forward, hands on either side of me, pulling my body down and his knee up. He connects underneath my ribs. I double over, teeth clenching to bite back the howl of pain as Rick's punishment continues, his fist striking a downward blow onto the back of my head. I fall to my knees, thinking of Tessa, of Beth's cold heart, of Matt, Chopper, and the penance the club owes for all of it. My body might be broken but my will isn't. I'm not out of this fight yet. "Killing me won't clean your slate, Rick. You'll always be the boy who cried because he couldn't hack it as a wolf."

I muster all I have left, coming up off the floor with a fist to Rick's groin. The impact jars him. I follow my momentum, driving my body up and straight through Rick's. He lands on his back. I hammer a fist downward. He eats the punch and catches my face between his palms, drawing me forward. Our skulls collide. My limbs go slack, eyes blinking against the haze. Rick flips me over, thick thighs straddling up high on my chest so I can't get enough power back to knock him off. He returns my hammer fist and I buck, shoving an elbow up his middle and connecting with the underside of his ribs. I know what that feels like and I'm happy to share the experience with him. He slams his forearm into my throat, leaning his weight forward until I can't even gasp for the air he's cutting off. "Randy wants to talk to a live Gripr, not a dead one. So watch your mouth and say please, and I'll let you keep breathing." His jaw ticks. "We have Tessa. Chief isn't as good at hiding her as you are."

~15~

Rick had me at the mention of Tessa's name. Unlike the woman herself, I'm predictable. The whole club knows it so I'm not surprised Rick played that card to end the fight. I'm not even surprised he has a key to Tessa's Highlander. The club drove it more than she did. From the time Gary rode into Hinton with the Leidolf, Tessa and everything she had was theirs.

When she and I first split, I liked that the club escorted her everywhere. Right up to the point when I realized they were keeping her away from me instead of keeping her safe *for* me. "If you're going to drive like you're ninety, pull over. I can walk to Randy faster than this."

Rick chuckles, the humor quickly fading from the sound. "You're right about Tessa. I failed her, and I'll take my due for the hurt I caused the same way the two of you will take yours. You're done running. Don't make me have to chase you again or I'll follow the order Gary gave and put you down."

I watch the road ahead of us, taking in all the possibilities of where we could be heading. "Gary is dead, so get yourself a new way of thinking because his way of doing things nearly got all of us killed right along with him."

Rick speeds up. "Keep talking, big man."

"I intend to," I snap. "I sat in church with all of you before I was even one of you and I told you I don't know how many times that the murders had nothing to do with club retaliation! None of you listened. Because of Gary. As much as I don't want to speak ill of the dead, Hinton went soft because of *Gary*." I glare at the side of Rick's face. "You didn't do your job because you were too busy playing with doctors, following Gary's lazy lead and acting like no one would dare come up against the mighty Leidolf. Well guess what, they did! And if I wouldn't have to listen to Tessa's mouth about it, I'd put a bullet in your head because I hold you solely responsible for letting that trash move in right next door. Matt should have been dead before he ever got to look at her."

Rick swerves hard, banging my head off the side window. "No one's playing anymore, Gripr, and you have more than your fair share of penance to pay, same as me. And some of our brothers aren't going to be as sweet to you as I was."

~

Tessa

Voices echo off the hillside. Chief was right about half of his men being used as guards at Mayor Smith's house. I'd forgotten that Possum was even on the police force until I saw him at the gate. Ever since Chief told him to let us in and to send out the order that the Leidolf walking through the front door were welcome by the mayor, I've been trying to remember Possum's real name. It should be an easy thing. Warren and I are the only ones who ever called the pinched-face boy by that name. Still, I can't recall what name anyone else uses.

I'd like to blame my memory loss on the shock that's still holding onto my senses, but I know the truth lies in what Warren told me on the mountain. I ignore everyone and everything. Not intentionally. I just never wanted to get mixed up in anyone else's drama. My whole life, all I've wanted is to live wild and free, the way Warren and I forced our lives to be. Things were always easy when it was just the two of us. We never had problems until other people came around and created them.

Chief's men give us space as we enter Mayor's house. I want to tell Randy to give me the same kind of space, but his body language tells me that request will be denied. He doesn't trust me anymore. None of them do. Warren doesn't even trust me. Rightly so. "Is..." I swallow, my words soft for only Randy to hear. "Are there others left alive? Or is who I saw tonight all that's left?"

His head tilts, coming closer to mine as our feet plod over the tile of the long hallway. "You'd know if you didn't run from us, but you ran off with the pup. How'd that work out for you?"

I should hold my tongue but I can't. Warren's hardly a pup. "If it wasn't for Montrose's charter, it would have worked out nicely. Has that situation been handled or should I be worried about getting burned out of this mansion?"

Randy looks down at me. "You should be worried about me."

I shiver. "All I'm worried about is Warren because the only thing he's guilty of is loving the wrong person. He doesn't deserve to be punished for my sins. Let him go, or let him take his rightful place in the club because there has never been a truer wolf than Warren."

The lines around Randy's eyes deepen, like etchings in stone. "This isn't the time or place. We'll all get our shot at airing out our grievances. Until then, keep your mouth shut."

I do as he says, focusing on the walls around us instead of on my fear for Warren's life. Mayor's house is by far nicer than anything else in Hinton. I wonder if he got some of his money from selling that porn he was making in the back of his Christian bookstore. The good Lord knows he didn't earn enough for a house this fancy on his meager salary from Hinton, even with those Bible sales on the side.

Chief flings open two heavy wooden doors, marching into a room set at the northern corner of the house. Two large windows flank a fireplace with a furry white rug in front of it. My stomach churns. Some people would call that fancy but one look at the crimson drapes over those windows tells me Mayor has an active fantasy life. I can see him filming one of the videos Warren told me about right here, with a woman on that rug and the flames of hell licking behind them.

I follow Chief's path, turning away from the fireplace and staying by Randy's side as Zeno falls back to guard the door. Mayor is at a polished wood desk that's facing the fireplace. I imagine he does quite a bit of daydreaming from here. Right now, his eyes are saucers. He's staring at Randy instead of Chief. "What...what's this all about? I was just turning in for the night."

Chief leans onto the desk, making the mayor look at him. "I know who our killers are. I just took out one of them and I need the manpower to go after the only one that's left."

Mayor's eyes flick to Randy again. "Okay. We have help from the state police and FBI already. Get what you need from them and pick up... Who did you *take out*? Who's behind these murders?"

"My sister," I answer for Chief.

Mayor chokes on his own spit, cheeks turning pink. "What? Beth? Impossible!"

Bile rises up my throat. That blush of his makes me think there's a video of him out there ramming himself into my sister's backside. "Tell your disbelief to Erin and her son. The person Chief handled was Arnold, Beth's boyfriend. He raped Erin's little boy and while he was doing it, Beth put a bag over that child's head. That was after she sliced open his mother, and then she left while Arnold continued to abuse a dead child."

Mayor's chin quivers. "Erin from Riverside Grille? That girl with the mysterious baby? Last I heard, she's no longer in Hinton. She left to avoid the shame of having that child."

Chief straightens, hooking his thumbs through his service belt. "Erin left to give herself a better life, and what Tessa just told you is all true. Beth has been operating a pedophile ring right under all of our noses. I don't know how deep it goes but I aim to find out. I need Hinton placed on lockdown. I want perimeters set, teams on four-wheelers, and units on every road from here to the edge of town. No one gets in or out. Order people to stay in their houses because we're sweeping every inch of this town from woods to private residences. Every house is getting searched and every locked door broken down. We're cleaning house."

Mayor's head shakes. "What you're asking for is worse than the governor declaring martial law. I've been doing my fighting best to get him to do that but he's resistant." Mayor's eyes dart to Randy. "Can't you find this one girl?"

Randy nods and the mayor lets out a sigh of relief, waving his hand at Randy. "There you have it, Chief. Take these bikers and use them for what you need."

Chief jerks his thumbs from his belt and rounds Mayor's desk. "With or without them, you're locking this town down. Now." He shoves the desk phone toward Mayor. "Call the news station and make the announcement."

My heart aches for Chief. Seeing his son murdered, hearing Arnold's awful words, has pushed him over an edge I can't imagine him ever climbing back up. But these curfews are bad enough and though this is bound to tick Randy off even more, holding my tongue has never been my strong suit. "Chief, the Leidolf will find Beth and we won't run around victimizing people already terrorized by her to do it. You can go ahead and gather up your men and start celebrating. The club will take it from here." I meet Mayor's stare. "Call that into the news if you like, let Hinton know the Leidolf will be patrolling their streets and cleaning their houses."

Randy shifts beside me. "She's speaking truth. We've been forced to clean our own house and now we'll clean up Hinton."

Chief spins away, muttering curses and glaring at Randy, then back at Mayor. "I'm trying to get a killer off the streets and I don't think you want to be known as the mayor who partnered with murderers and fire starters instead of your own police force!"

"You're one to talk." I remind Chief of the brains he had me wearing like a full face of makeup. I chance marching away from Randy, splaying my palms over the cool surface of Mayor Smith's desk. "Do you know why it's so hard to live with secrets? People like Warren can lord them over your head."

Mayor slinks back in his chair, his proud shoulders doing their best not to sag under the weight of what he now knows that I know. If it means stopping this martial law nonsense, I'm not a bit above blackmail.

He stares at me, Chief kicking up a fuss beside where Mayor and I are sizing one another up. Commotion breaks at the door. I keep my eyes on Mayor until I hear Warren's voice. I spin, the room around me doing the same. Zeno moves to the side. Warren stumbles into the room, compliments of a hard shove from Rick. I race toward Warren. Randy catches me around the waist, doubling me over and forcing me back against him. Warren lets out a roar, his own body snagged between Rick and Zeno. "You hit her? You freaking hit her!"

I lift a hand to my busted face. My swollen eyes already had moons of black shining under them when I got out of Erin's shower, it's hard to say what color of bruised they are now. "No." I let them plead with Warren. "The club didn't do this. It was Arnold. He's working with Beth and we found him. Chief and me."

Warren's long finger points at Chief, and I know the tremble is from rage, not exhaustion or fear. "*You* did this. And I'm going to roast you on a spit like the pig you are."

Chief stomps toward him, hand too heavy on that service weapon. Rick and Zeno turn Warren loose and I fight Randy's grip. He lets me go and I run full force at Warren, slamming my hands out, one palm each landing on Warren and Chief's advancing chests. "No one's in the mood for barbecue and we're all on the same team here, so both of you are lowering your measuring sticks." I look between them. "We have a common enemy and she isn't in this room so we're all good now, right?"

Warren knocks my hand off his chest, clamping his fingers over my shoulder with a bruising grip. "We're far from good, but you're back where you belong so that's a start."

Rick snorts and Zeno rolls his eyes. I look to Randy. His eyes are trained on Chief and that grip he has on his unholstered weapon. I spin to Warren and throw my arms around his neck, pressing my lips to his ears. "We just found Erin and her boy murdered so cut Chief some slack before you get us both killed." I ball a handful of his scraggly hair in my fist. "You're not supposed to be here. You're supposed to be safe, healing up somewhere safe until I end this."

His arm circles my waist, crushing me against him. His other hand lifts to my face, barely touching the tips of his fingers to the tender side of my nose. "I know you have a hell of a lot of nerve, but I already told you how it was going to go if you tried to twist up a scenario so you can dump me again." He grips my chin. "No one touches you. That was the deal, and you broke it. Now your precious Chief gets to meet my inner demon, and mine's better than anything that ever possessed your little pet Chopper."

"Shut up, Gripr," Randy barks, moving toward us, backing Chief away.

Warren lifts his glare from me to Randy. "I'm not going to shut up until you take yourself a good look at her face right now. This damage is *your* handiwork as much as it's the pig's."

I loosen my grip on Warren's hair. "The only person responsible for my damage is dead, and I didn't break our deal. I left you to *deal* with your Marcie situation and if you'd done that, you wouldn't be here getting ready to have your brains blown out by our trigger-happy Chief."

Warren's eyes narrow. "No, you took the pig's bait and ran right out into a setup half-cocked because you never think before you act."

I take my arms from around his neck. "I assure you I was fully cocked."

"And I assure you," Mayor's voice soars over his desk, his chair creaking as he lifts out of it. "That what Chief is asking me for is extreme. With all of you working together, I think we can resolve what's ailed our Hinton this summer. Quickly. And outside of my home."

I crane my neck, making eye contact with Chief. He turns away. This time I feel his tension thicken, amping and brittle all at the same time. I clutch Warren, trying to force him down, my words coming out too slow. "Move!" I shout, but Mayor's blood is already splattered across the room, what's left of his head resting on his desk.

Randy returns the fire now aimed at us, Chief holed up behind the thick wood of Mayor's expensive desk. "Officer down!" Chief shouts. "They killed him! The bikers killed Mayor Smith!"

~16~

Warren

The hand I already have clamped onto the back of Tessa's shirt tightens, my grip dragging her to the door with me. Mayor Smith's death was bound to come, and by unnatural means. The man was involved in too many dirty deeds for his life to end any other way. I just expected his end to play out differently, coming at the hands of a jealous lover or those of his wife. Not from the barrel of Chief's gun.

"Move!" I parrot Tessa's words. Rick brought me here in case I was needed in negotiations, the club knowing I have dirt on the mayor without knowing the exact nature of said dirt. Whatever deal they thought they'd be working out, they didn't bargain on Chief going rogue. Or on him having the guts to frame the club.

I duck Tessa through the door with me, covering her head as we fall in behind Zeno. He moves swiftly, an arsenal all his own between the guns he carries and the throwing knives he's deadly with. A darn good thing considering Chief doesn't intend for any of us to get off this property alive. He used Tessa to set the club up. When he left with her, he knew they'd find her, and he'd be there when they did. He wanted credit for bringing down the Leidolf. A side effect of being on record as the first lawman to arrest a club member, a feat he earned only because of Gary's bad judgment.

I push Tessa's head further down, eyes on the end of the hall where our exit is. Shaun is out there, but so are a whole team of pigs. "Happy now?" I snap at Tessa, glancing back to Randy and Rick. I'm unarmed. Rick left my rifle behind when he dragged me out of my own garage, so him covering my rear is the least he can do. Cops are filing into the house, having been standing in wait for Chief's signal.

If it wasn't for the numbers against us, Randy wouldn't have just clipped Chief, he would have made sure his next shot found its deadly mark. As it stands, if we hesitate, we die. I swing back to Tessa and push her harder, keeping her feet moving just as quickly as Zeno's. Chief might spare her life but she's seen enough of her men die. She doesn't need another dead wolf on her conscience and these bullets slinging around us don't care who they hit. I'm particularly partial to not only my own life but Tessa's.

We dart around a corner and I press her as close to Zeno's back as possible. There are guard pigs between us and those vehicles parked outside and I can only hope the gunfire we're heading for is Shaun clearing our way out.

Zeno throws the front door open and we race outside. Shaun is hunkered down on the corner, spraying bullets. "You're clear, and the wheels are hot."

Zeno drops down beside Shaun and motions us forward. I tuck Tessa's head under my armpit and dash for the Highlander, aching ribs be damned. Rick charges around us. I catch sight of Randy on my left. The men spread out to either side of the Highlander, returning fire and flinging open doors. There's blood trickling down Rick's arm and the sight of it stirs up a joy I shouldn't be feeling right now.

I shove Tessa through the door behind Randy with a rougher hand than necessary. I'm not going to worry about taking it easy on her until we're clear of the law and I have a gun of my own. "Scoot." I push her aside and scramble onto the backseat, flinging her down into the floorboard.

"Hey!" Her head cranks around, fire in her eyes.

I cup a palm around her skull and press her face down. She can be ticked but I'm going to do whatever it takes to keep her alive. "Our bad situation just got a heck of a lot worse, Tessa, all because of your pet piggy. So stay down and let the club get us out of a jam for once."

Rick hops behind the wheel, throwing the Highlander into reverse and looking over at Randy in the shotgun seat. "The pup is as arrogant as ever."

Randy grunts. "That makes me even more anxious for the others to reunite with him."

I dig the pills out of my pocket, throwing back a chalky tablet and crunching the foul-tasting pill between my teeth. I wrench my aching torso over the back of the seats. "Put your foot on the gas, Grandpa. I have a Chief Piggy power-tripping because he has a thing for my girl, and we don't want to let him make us late for our family reunion."

Tessa's fingers dig into my ankle hard enough to make me clamp my teeth together. "With any luck, we'll get to that reunion before you overdose. And Chief's *thing* is for you, not me." She turns me loose and fits herself between the two front seats. "Rick, if we make it out of this, call Dr. Lafferty. She loves you."

Sirens blare to life, police cars filling the roadway at the end of Mayor's long driveway. I throw open the cache and toss the contents, popping the bottom out of the box. I yank out the chest holster, slinging it over my shoulder and drawing one of the pistols. "Cops. Lots of them."

Rick swings the Highlander around and barrels down on them, Zeno and Shaun right behind us in their Subaru. Randy leans out his window, opening fire on the four police cars fanning out to box us in. I launch back over the seat and plant my palm on the top of Tessa's head. "Down!"

She slumps back into the floorboard and I spin to my own window, leaning out and firing at the tires of the closest car. Rick doesn't let off the accelerator. He holds the pedal down and cuts right when a cruiser shoots across our path. The Highlander crunches through the car's front end. Our tires hit the pavement and Rick lets out a whoop. "Come get us, piggies!"

Zeno slides onto the road behind us, Shaun raised out of their moonroof, laying down a spray of bullets that's taking out vehicle and man alike. Between his guns and Zeno's knives, I'm pretty sure those two could take on a small country, and I'd play the odds for them to win.

I drop back through my window. Tessa is still where I put her. I tug her arm to my lap, pressing her palm to my thigh as a way to anchor her to me. She looks up at me, the wild look in her blackened eyes making my stomach flip. "I don't want to die in a police shootout. Not until I kill my sister."

A bullet breaks through the back glass, shooting over my head and hitting the front windshield. I duck over her. "Just keep getting acquainted with your floormats and Marcie's wish for you to die won't come true. If I happen to die, I'm sure you won't have a problem trying your hand with another wolf."

Tessa's fingers climb up my leg, twitching over the gun dangling near my waistband. "Tell Marcie I already died, and that if this mob Chief is forming doesn't kill you too, I'll be raising from the dead to let her know how I feel about my name being in her mouth."

My heart flutters. This woman is a lightning strike and I'm a dang fool for her jolt. I place my hand over hers and ease her fingers down the gun, pinching back the one she has on the trigger. "Keep your hands off of guns, Tessa. You're a bad enough shot that Chief won't need his mob, you'll end up shooting all of us."

I right the holster and shove my arms through the loops. The gun she was trying to get her paws on lies heavy against my side. Randy ducks back into the vehicle. "Down!"

A blast lights up the rearview, the shockwave causing Rick to skid. He grips the wheel and drives out of it, Zeno racing up to flank our left. Shaun's muzzle flashes and another explosion rocks the road underneath us. I crank my neck. Blinding smoke is billowing up behind us.

Shaun drops down into the Subaru and both vehicles head straight for the woods. I yank Tessa up and wrap my arms around her. Rick slams the brakes, the back end of the Highlander sliding into a tree, throwing me against the door and banging Tessa's head against my chin.

"Are you trying to kill us?" I shout.

A lopsided grin jumps off his face. "Relax, Gripr. We're just having some fun."

I shove my door open and pull Tessa out with me, gluing my hand to her and running us in the direction of Randy's fading shadow. Rick goes to Zeno, unloading ammo and weapons from the Subaru while Shaun fires another decimating round, that under-barrel launcher sending a grenade cartridge out into the road behind us, cutting off access for any law enforcement still stupidly in pursuit.

Tessa trips, dragging me down with her. "Darn it, woman! Pick up your feet!"

Her arms wrap around my neck, her mouth rushing to my ear. "Run, Warren. Hide in the smoke. I'll distract the club...convince them to leave you here."

My teeth clench to the point of breaking. "You'd like that, but I'm not a coward. Our chances are better with the club so I'm sticking to them and you're sticking to me." I lower into her face. "No one but *me*. No place but at *my* side. *Nothing* in your head except for *me*."

Her eyes widen. "Please, Warren, don't do this. Be angry with me but don't hand yourself over to a battle you can't win."

I peel us off the ground and tug her back into motion. "Lucky for me, I don't need you to believe in me to win my battles."

She tugs on my arm. "Now who's half-cocked? You can't take on our entire charter."

I spin and jam a finger into her face. "I've been tricked already, Tessa. Thinking the whole time that if I couldn't have you, at least you were being looked after by the best. It was all a lie. Now there's hell to pay and I'm the bill collector."

"Warren," she growls.

Shaun races up behind her, his arm snaking around her middle. I clamp my free hand over her shoulder and rip her back toward me. "There's no way in hell I'm giving Tessa to you. Turn her loose. This is the only time I'll ask so nicely."

Tessa pushes on my chest. "I'll go with—"

"No!" I grind.

Zeno rushes forward. "Let her go, Shaun. They both know they belong to us, so let our she-wolf have one last ride with our Gripr."

Shaun shoves her into me and Tessa's nails dig into my hand. We take off after Zeno, running until our feet break out onto a trail. One so old that trees have reclaimed most of it. The summer foliage is thick and hiding a beautiful sight. My bikes. All of them. Motorcycles, four-wheelers, dirt bikes, and even a scooter I picked up at the salvage yard for Norma Kay. A few of the ladies in her trailer park have them and I saw Samantha's mom eyeing their rides so I decided to fix this one up for her. I plan to paint it the bright colors she likes and fancy it up until it's worthy of the envy of all those women who like to gossip about Norma Kay's daughter.

"Chief said he impounded my rides?" I ask Randy. He's already sitting atop a four-wheeler, Rick on one right beside him.

Randy's eyes stay on Tessa. "We picked up what belongs to us."

I yank Tessa away from him and pull her to my favorite dirt bike. "Get on, and put your arms around me like you mean for them to be there."

She scrambles onto the bike, Zeno climbing onto the back of Rick's and Shaun jumping on Randy's. I mount my bike and Tessa's arms squeeze around my waist. "I'm a mean drunk and you're an idiot when you're high, so let's make a pact to both stop abusing substances."

I kick the bike to life. "Nah. You're just plain mean, so even if I did get off the drugs, you'd still be you, so I'm keeping the dope."

~17~

The club set more than one trap for Tessa and me, Chief being the link that got them to her and Rick being the lucky wolf who picked the right spot and lay in wait for me the longest. Wherever the others might have been, all their plans led to exactly where we ended up. A defensible and isolated stretch of road peppered with escape routes and littered with bikes connected to me, their new patch-in. If the stash had been found, especially the ones they broke out of impound after Chief picked them up, I was the only wolf on the hook.

The only other thing I'm sure of is that Rick came on strong, but he wasn't looking for the kill. Randy's doing. A decision I'm sure my new leader isn't firm on. I'm not firm on my decision to be riding along behind him either, but the club is currently our best shot at survival. I can handle Beth. If she's dumb enough to come for either of us, she's going to die feeling what Teresa felt when that little girl lost her life. But shaking loose of the club while avoiding the law and the strays isn't something I'm physically capable of right now, if I ever could manage such a feat to begin with.

I race behind Randy's bike, toward the lights I looked at from this same patch of woods not long ago. Tessa's arms are wrapped tightly around me, the occasional twitch of her fingers against my stomach relaying her fear. I stick close to the dust Randy is kicking up. There's no stopping at the edge of the pavement to scour the parking lot of Town's End. We roll across the pavement and straight through the open doors of my largest bay, Carl standing there waiting for us.

I skid my bike to a stop and pull Tessa off it. She moves toward Randy. I rake a hand through her hair and tug it into my first. "Not just yet. We have some things to talk about."

I give her hair a good yank for spite. Her eyes shoot daggers through me but she clamps her mouth shut and comes where I lead. The last bike skids past us. Shaun jumps off the back. "This way, Gripr."

I keep stomping across the floor, away from where Carl is closing the bay door and past where Randy and the others are heading up the stairs to my office. "You go whatever direction you want. Straight down into hell would be a good one. But give me your gun before you go, it would be a shame to lose a piece like that."

"Shh," Tessa hisses, halfheartedly fighting my grip on her hair.

I veer toward the partition in the back of the garage. "I'll shush once you agree to all the groveling you're going to be doing for years to come. Maybe for the rest of our lives because you have a lot of memories to wash out of my head."

"Gripr." Randy's voice echoes across the empty expanse of garage. "Tessa doesn't belong to you, she's *ours*. Your first loyalty is to *us*, not her. We deal with the sister, the cops, the rest of Montrose's stray dogs, and then I personally deal with you."

I turn and face him, bringing Tessa around with me. I meet the stare of each man beside him, tightening my grip on her, a mix of sentiment reading in the set of their jaws and the narrowed glint of their eyes. They're ticked at both of us, but they don't like her being manhandled. Not by me. "She's *mine*. No one touches her but *me*. So while *I* deal with *her*, the rest of you can back off. I'm going to give her a nice soft place to stew while she reconsiders her life choices." I meet Randy's eyes. "Try taking her from me again and I'll be using this to even the battlefield." I draw my knife free of its sheath. "It's only fair, considering what you sent Chopper to do to me."

"I missed him," Zeno says with too much of a grin in his voice. One that says what he misses is beating me down.

I shove my knife back into its sheath. "On second thought, I don't need a weapon. It's long past time for all of you to learn your lessons and once I give this woman of mine hers, I'll give each of you a turn at kissing my rosy cheeks because that's as close as any of you will ever get to Tessa again."

Rick leans on the banister. "Don't leave out our brothers from our Northern Charter. Bear always did say he liked the curve of the Gripr's cheeks."

I flip him off and turn back to my course, dragging Tessa across the space with the ease of familiarity, slipping us behind the partition blocking our van from view. She inhales, a sharp sound that gives my frayed nerves a hit of satisfaction. There was a big chance the club wouldn't give me this time with her. They could have stomped me just now and ripped her right out of my hands. I couldn't show them weakness though, and Tessa's are the only feet I'll ever beg at. Right now, I'd like to clamp her feet in shackles and chain her to the inside of this van she's looking at like it just popped out of the smoke Shaun and his grenades kicked up.

I shove her forward. "I'm a rat, remember? And rats pack things away while scurrying all over town making holes so they can get away anytime they need to." I throw open the van door. "A rat's skills come in real handy when his woman is an idiot who doesn't know how to do as she's told."

She jerks toward me but I'm ready for this fight. I push her backward until she's pinned against the side of the van and my hands are clamped around her wrists. "The thing about pain pills is that they let you forget your insides are smashed up. You're not getting by me again."

"I'm not trying to get by you," she seethes. "I'm trying to save you!"

I pull her off the van and shove her toward the open door. "Before your mouth runs off with any more of the lies your head is filled with, I suggest you have a seat."

She climbs through the open door and crawls up between the front seats. I follow her, twisting my fingers into the back of her shirt and yanking. She knows good and well where I meant for her to sit. "Don't you freaking dare." I fold down onto the bed, bringing her with me. "You've been on a crash course since the day you put an inch of space between us and you running out Chief's door earned you a head-on collision with me."

"Fine, Warren." She plops into my lap, harder than necessary, eyes calling out the flicker of pain I couldn't keep from curling up my lip. "Is this what you want? Marcie wasn't good enough crawling around on you so you need me to do it too? Or do you prefer to hear that I *am* glad that you always snuck around for us, stealing whatever food we needed and even spending all summer lugging rocks up a mountain just to build us a private little firepit in that cave we claimed as our own? You tell me exactly what it is you want from me because this isn't the summer of love and you're the one being an idiot!"

I clamp my fingers up around either side of her face, cradling her chin in my palm, forcing her eyes to stay locked on mine. I know there's something wrong with me, something worse than the pain-numbing drugs currently doing a number on my senses, but the fire in this woman turns me on like nothing else can. "I gave you *years* to get your crap together and you couldn't wait on me for a single day? I didn't ask for Marcie to show up at Chief's house but she did, and I couldn't turn her away like I never cared about her because I did. I *do*. Which is no different than how your relationship with Chopper was. You cared about him and you wouldn't just toss him aside."

"That's why I didn't ask you to toss Marcie out!" she screams. "I left you with her, Warren, so your body could heal and you could take your time dealing with all the feelings you have for her, but I wasn't going to sit around and watch her rub you in my face."

The rage holding court in my chest right now is tempting me to rub quite a few things in Tessa's face. She made me watch her give herself to Chopper and I should return the favor. But Tessa didn't know I was there on that riverbank, and I won't use Marcie as a means of getting even. She deserves better. And my sick little self loves the fact that Tessa is jealous as hell.

I spread my fingers up through her hair and twist it into a loose fist at the nape of her neck. "What you did was look me in the eye and lie right to my face. If Chopper never died on that mountain, would you have ever again said you loved me? Or would you have run off with him and never thought twice about whether I was dead or alive?"

Her lips part, voice rattling. "I would have cared whether you were dead or alive even when I was pretending I didn't, and I was wholly yours again before Chopper ever showed up on the mountain. All I had to do was see myself in the mirror of your eyes, the very thing I avoided doing because deep down I always knew I was just a scared little girl running from the one thing I truly wanted because I didn't believe myself worthy of being loved by you." Her eyes track the shadows in mine. "I didn't lie to you, Warren. I *will* go where you go and I'll fight for you above all others."

"Right," I huff. "You'll go where I go until it suits you to do something different."

She reaches back and closes my fist around the tight ball of her hair. "I'll ride for you just like I'll die for you, but I'm not worth the spit you're wasting on arguing with me and if you keep acting like I am, you're going to lose more than only Marcie. You're going to lose your life, Warren. I ran from you so you'd have a chance. At least for a little while."

"You ran from me because you wanted to," I shout.

She loosens her grip and lets her hand fall to her lap. "You're right. I ran because I wanted to. I wanted to leave you when you had someone else's arms to be in. Someone you dreamed up a future with the way we used to dream of ours." Her throat works. "As much as it hurt, I left because I knew that if I didn't make it back to you, you'd still have a dream to live because the difference between Marcie and me is that you actually have a future with her." She lifts watery eyes to mine. "You don't deserve to be punished for my stupid choices and Marcie is the only person who ever had a real shot at taking your love from me. I know because of all the people I heard you'd been out with, she's the one who made my stomach tighten. The only good thing was that it had the decency to wait until I was alone before it spewed up everything I'd put in it the day you walked out of a movie theater holding Marcie's hand for all of Hinton to see."

I tighten my grip, pulling her face closer to mine. "You running away from me didn't make anything better, it made it all worse. Just like before. Aren't you tired of doing this by now?"

"Aren't you tired of running for your life by now?" she retorts. "You came after me even though you know you can't win a gun fight let alone a hand-to-hand battle, and you challenged every wolf left alive!"

I drop my hand from her hair to the small of her back. "If the club wanted me dead, I'd be dead. But getting rid of me isn't on their agenda the way me getting rid of them is on mine. For letting that scumbag neighbor get close enough to put hands on you, Rick is getting knocked out first and he'll be lucky if I don't gut him."

Her jaw ticks. "Rick didn't *let* Matt put hands on me, *I* did! Me, Warren, *me*. The very first night I was with Matt it only happened because I ran from the club. After that, they let it happen because I fought them every time they told me no. You're laying sins at feet they don't belong at. I did this." She jabs her finger into her chest, harder with each word. "Me. Me. Me, me, me, me--"

I grab her jabbing finger and squeeze it to a stop. "I know the part you played and the partners who played you. It was easily done, considering you started losing your ever-loving mind about three years ago. That's when I lost mine, too. I handed it straight over to a pack of wolves who kicked me in the teeth and swore *they'd* be the ones making sure your life was happy and full. I'll hold them accountable for that failure just as hard as they plan to hold us accountable for all that we've done. I'll lay any darn thing I like at their feet while you stand behind me so they can look at what they might as well have done to you themselves."

"Only they didn't do it," she spits. "And you've gone from barely getting out of bed to being a hyperactive child. Adrenaline and drugs, Warren, you've got it all running through your system and you're not thinking straight."

She's partly right. My head is messed up enough that my heart is riding on my lips more than I care for it to. "There were times when I always knew I was your choice, Tess. I want so badly for you to make me believe that's what I am again."

Her fingers thread along my face and into my hair. "You are. It's always been you, Warren. That's why seeing you moving on with Marcie hurt so much. All I ever managed to do was make everyone else believe I moved on too. I hid my true feelings, sometimes even from myself."

I narrow my eyes on her. "Then why is it so hard for you to keep your promises to me?"

She lets go of me and wipes her eyes. "You could always make something out of nothing and you always put us first. You're the glue that mends all the things I break, and I break a lot of things because all I'm good for is messing up both of our lives. I don't deserve you, Warren."

A little stab of guilt eats at me. She's only responsible for a third of what's gone wrong in our lives, and half of that third is because I hung her out to dry. I was still a boy three years ago. Now I've had my right of passage. When Gary loaned me the money for this garage, I was already through the trials and on my way to becoming a man prepared for everything, because I knew Gary's loan had strings and when he pulled them, I had to be ready.

I drag Tessa's mouth to mine and drink my relief straight from the source. "You haven't deserved me in recent years, Tess, but you did in the past. Not a person in this town doubted that you'd walk through fire for me. Then you suddenly wouldn't, and it shocked everyone, especially me." I rest my forehead on hers. "Then we were put into an actual fire and we both walked out of it and straight to each other. So yeah, I'm going to give you hell for what you put me through these past years, but I won't forget that you broke yourself in the process, too. Now stop crying and kiss me. I want to do a few things with you before these pills wear off because I'm not playing with glue anymore, baby. I'm using truckloads of cement."

~18~

Tessa

Making love to Warren is satisfying, like rainfall on parched earth. Deep, penetrating, and soul-healing. Despite knowing the club could drag us out of this van at any second, we're both taking our time with each other, the pace agonizing as we reclaim what was ours. Everything is new in this experience because there was never anyone between us before. My body was his, and his mine. "I love you, Warren," I rasp as he feathers kisses over my skin, as thorough with loving every inch of me as he ever was.

"I know," he growls. "I'm making sure you never forget that again."

I twist my fists into the comforter stretched over the piece of foam in the back of our van, surrounded by a home on wheels that looks the same today as it did the last time I made love to him in the back of it. Save for the gun tucked down beside the foam bedding and the two-gun holster hanging over the back of the driver's seat. "I never forgot anything. And it doesn't feel like you did either."

A smile breaks over his lips. "Plenty of the Leidolf are wifed up, Tess, and those women are just fine. Mine will be too. *Both* of them."

I curl my fingers through his scruffy hair. "You're the most special thing on this side of forever, Gripr, and I'm not sharing you with anyone so you better start making mine the only name you know."

~

I run my fingers across Warren's chest, nestled in the crook of his arm, feeling as if we erased everything bad between us and put ourselves back together again. I rest my palm over his heart. "I can't believe you kept our van. When you stopped driving it, I just assumed you finally found another place to take your dates."

His lips press against my temple. "I never let anyone in here. I couldn't. By the time I realized you had every intention of moving on, I could barely bring myself to do anything other than just sit in here and curse your name."

My heart constricts. "I'm sorry I was so scared and childish for all these years."

He pulls in a breath. "We were both childish, Tess. The only difference is that I was never scared. Not of you. Us. We were the only thing I was ever sure of and when you took that away from me, I handled it like a boy."

I sit up. "Or maybe you handled it like you should have. I'm still me, Warren. Maybe the reason I was able to break us so easily is because you figured out who I really am and the man growing inside of you knew I was a bad choice."

He runs a hand down my spine. "I've always known who you are, Tess. You're the girl who thought you had to use other people to get under my skin when all it ever took was your hand in mine to get a rise out of me. Now you're the woman who is still doing stupid things in the heat of the moment, all because you love people, especially me." He tugs me back to his chest. "I'm not your collateral damage anymore. I'm the vinegar to your oil. Now stop talking because we're great together and we haven't finished breaking our van back in yet."

My hand molds to the curve of his jaw, body freezing at the sound of a ping echoing from out in the garage. "They're coming for us, and you have to let Randy take me. You can't fight them, Warren. Promise me."

His fingers dig into my arm. "Get dressed."

I open my mouth to protest but a shot rings out. I tug my shirt over my head. "Who's shooting?"

Warren puts a finger to his lips and shoves his legs through his battle-scared cargo pants. We heard a four-wheeler leave earlier but the garage has been quiet ever since. Well, outside of the noise we made inside this van.

Warren takes pills from his pocket and tosses a couple into his mouth, chewing them like gum. I frown at him. He shoves my pants at me and reaches for the gun holster, strapping it around his bare chest. I lean into him. "In case I haven't said it enough in the last couple of hours, I love you, Gripr, and I'm *so* proud of you. You've always been so much more than anyone ever wanted to give you credit for but the man I see before me is the one I always knew you were."

He raises his hand, lowering all of his fingers except for one. "Don't go soft on me now, *Mrs*. Gripr. Just put your pants on and replace those stars in your eyes with hatred because I need the pissed-off Tessa right now." He kisses me. "This is war, baby. If I wanted a gush fest I would have brought Marcie with me."

Sorrow billows through me. Warren's never been one to hold his tongue but in the last few years, I made him hold it. That alone robs me of the right to be called his wife, even in jest. What belongs to me is the hatred I bred in him. I tug on my pants and reach for the gun tucked into the cushion. "I promise I won't shoot you this time."

His jaw clenches. "I've heard that before."

I cup my hand over the lever on the van door. "Let me go first, then I won't accidentally shoot you. We don't even know who's out there anyway, it could be someone on our side who doesn't need shooting."

He presses his hand overtop of mine. "Just because I rocked your world doesn't mean you have to start protecting me. Stay behind me and move when I do. If I stop, duck, and don't take that gun off of safety unless I'm dead."

He shoves the door open and pulls me out with him, leaving the van wide open as we ease toward the edge of the partition. He curls an arm around me, pressing me into his back. I peek over his shoulder, scanning the bay ahead of us. Warren stops, but I don't duck. Skulking along the edge of the oil pit is a shadow that makes my blood run cold. Every time Lad showed up with Montrose I found myself questioning how he fit into the Northern Charter's ranks. He's shorter than most women I know and built like a troll, his face twisted to match his stalky body and too-wide shoulders. He's unlike every other wolf I've ever met and I never figured he was Leidolf stealthy. I guess I'm right about that since his bulky feet are sending another bolt pinging into the pit.

Warren's head cocks to the side and I follow his line of sight. Another man is descending the stairs. "Gene," I whisper.

Warren nods, his hand unlatching from my body and coming up to the side of his head where my face is. He holds up three fingers and points to his right, telling me that on the count of three, he wants me to run. Considering the blood oozing out from where Carl's head is resting on the bottom step, I'm guessing Warren is right that these wolves are stray. I nuzzle my nose into the hair by his ear. "You better be right behind me."

His hand curls into a fist. He flicks one finger up, hesitating only a second before he adds a second one to the count. I click the safety off on my gun. He tenses, halting the rise of the third finger. It flings up next to the others and I run for the side of the garage, using the two huge toolboxes for cover. Footsteps pound across the floor. Not Warren's.

A shot rings out, followed by two more. Warren yells. I skid to a halt and spin around. Gene is lying in a pool of blood beside Carl but Lad is on top of Warren, his lump of a body pinning Warren's frame to the ground. I run toward them, pointing my gun at the writhing mass of men. Warren's neck screws itself around, bringing his eyes to mine. "Don't you dare shoot, woman!"

"Then you shoot him," I yell.

Lad's face darts in my direction. Warren elbows him between the eyes, his long sinewy muscles wrapping around Lad's torso. His hands are empty. I glance around for his gun, the two of them grappling for position in a way Warren isn't ready for yet. Those pills might dull his pain but they're not healing him up inside.

I drop to my knees and shove my hand underneath a tire rack. "Run, Tessa!" Warren shouts at me.

"Not unless you can reach your gun!" I shout back.

Warren lets out a roar. I draw my hand back and pivot in his direction. Lad has his fat hand on Warren's throat. I take aim. Warren's eyes fly wide but his hands are trapped between Lad and his own stomach so it's not like I can pass him this weapon. "Close your eyes."

Warren throws his head forward, butting his skull against Lad's. Blood blooms between them. Warren rams his knee up, flipping Lad, and like a cat instead of a wolf, he pounces. His elbows batter Lad's face. Lad rolls. Warren jumps onto his back, shoving a forearm under the troll's neck and locking the man's head in a bruising choke, his arms squeezing until his muscles are near to busting. His eyes lock on mine, Lad's hands clawing at his throat, mouth sputtering and head swelling as blood pools in his face. Warren leans him forward, stretching Lad out and tucking his heels against the inside of the man's thighs until Lad is flat on his stomach. Warren's arms pull back and up, every drop of drug and adrenaline inside him keeping the pressure on Lad's neck until the man's hands fall away limp, his body still under Warren.

Warren lets him go, shoving up off him. I stare at Lad. "Is he dead?"

Warren coughs, spewing bloody spit across Lad's back. "I'm okay, Tess. Thanks for asking."

I move to his side. "You're alive, but you're not okay. I already know those two things so I don't need to ask."

His chest heaves and he stomps to the tire rack I'd just been searching under. He shoves his arm up under the end of it and withdraws his gun, nostrils flaring and mouth sucking air. He stomps back and aims the barrel at Lad. He pumps two bullets into the back of Lad's head. "Now he's dead. And I guess the club is too since they let these fleabags get to us."

My eyes float to Carl, and then up the stairs Gene was descending when Warren shot him. The stairs where I last saw Randy, Zeno, and Rick. I run for the steps, grabbing the banister and jumping over Gene's body. "They're not up there, Tess," Warren calls from below me. "We would have heard the shots."

I stay my course, racing into Warren's office. It's empty. I lean against the wall, gulping air and slowing my breathing. Warren ducks into the room beside me, drug-hazed eyes gleaming even in the dimness of the room. He tips the gun out the door, toward the corner of the garage he'd told me to run to. "Start listening to me, woman. We need to get out of here. If Gene and Lad found us, the rest of the strays can too." He fists a hand into the front of my shirt. "And don't you ever point a gun at me again."

~19~

I traipse along beside Warren. It's easier to fight with him than worry about what happened to Randy and the others. "If I'd been in a fight with Lad, you wouldn't have run either."

Warren cracks open the slender door on the side of the garage, looking out into the parking lot between us and the Snack Shack. He pushes the door fully open and reaches for my hand. "I don't need to run because I know how to shoot, unlike you. So if I tell you to stay put, stay. If I tell you to run, run. I'm not asking you to pilot a rocket ship here, Tessa."

I glare at where he's leading us. To the house he's building. For *Marcie*. "If you want a woman who will do as she's told, go put Marcie on the back of your bike and run off into that sunrise that's just about to break over the mountain."

"Keep it up and I just might," he grumbles.

I suck my tongue back into my mouth. Bickering is comforting for us but those piercing fingers of guilt are gripping my heart. Nothing I do ever works out in anyone's favor, especially Warren's. Yet he's the one next to me. And after I got rid of nearly everything that belonged to him because even the smallest reminders were too hard to cope with seeing. I only kept items that I could tuck away and not come across unexpectedly. Like his clothes that were packed into the back of my closet and the beads he gave me that are in my jewelry box with Samantha's necklace. I don't wear jewelry often and rarely open that box of keepsakes, and here Warren is living with me all around him. He saved every scrap of memory we made together and kept our van, even with a different woman living in his house.

In a way, he's like Gary. Rugged on the outside and soft as a day-old kitten on the inside. "Warren, I meant what I said. If something happens to me, I want you to be happy with Marcie. But only in this life. You're mine in every other one because I'm going to need the rest of eternity to love you the way I should have always been doing."

"It's going to take us longer than eternity to make up and we're not giving up on this life just yet." He faces me, snaking an arm around my waist and pulling me against him. "You make me happy, Tess. Always have. Even in times when there shouldn't be an ounce of happiness to be had. I'm sorry if I didn't give that back to you. I'm sorry that this life we're living right now isn't on the same plane of existence as all the dreams we had. But this is what we've got." His lips press against the swollen side of my nose. "Today is not the day we die, baby, so just listen to me because there's someone coming through the brush on our left. I need you to run for the river. I dug a deep hole out there for us so just swim out to the middle and wait for me. If who swims out for you isn't me, drown them."

~

Warren

The closest I came to dying during the fight with Lad was Tessa slinging that gun of hers around. Now I'm going to come close again because she's running all right, but toward who's coming through the brush instead of away from him. Of all the Leidolf I've seen so far, Shaun is the one showing the least amount of self-control. Him plying the cops with that friendly reminder earlier doesn't mean he's loyal to the club. The pigs in this town were owed what they got. Leidolf and stray alike would agree that no one walks into our house and stands against us.

I clutch at Tessa. "Get behind me, woman."

"It's Shaun," she huffs.

I yank her to a stop. "My eyes are working just fine, I can see who it is. Just like I can see you doing the exact opposite of what I asked you to do."

She steps into me. "You didn't ask, you ordered, and if you don't like me trying to save your hide, remember that you could be with Marcie right now."

I draw my gun. "I could, but I'd rather be here watching your jealous backside climb into that river than be in her bed. Get down to that shoreline, Tessa."

I whirl around to where Shaun's boots are storming toward us, one big gun strapped to his back and another held tight in front of him. "Friend or foe? Tell me quick because there are two dead strays and a wolf in my garage and I'm real tired of getting punched in the face."

Shaun's eyes dart to the path we just ran down. "Carl?"

"Dead."

He looks between Tessa and me and then down at the gun in my hand. "Montrose's charter?"

I spit off to the side and wipe a hand across my mouth. "If you're asking who did the killing, I don't know who shot Carl but I took care of Gene and Lad. Now I'll ask you again to tell me if I should be working on putting a bullet in you too because while I appreciate the privacy, I didn't expect the club to run off on us."

Shaun steps forward. "You got privacy because we're busy, and I'm looking forward to the day you try to put a bullet in me."

I'd like to make today that day but he knows as well as everyone that though I'd fight him even with my limbs missing, Tessa is my weakness. I'm not going to attack a man who can help me get her away from the paws of Montrose's mutts. "Where are the others?"

"On their way," he answers with a smirk I'm itching to wipe off his face. "I put in the call and left Carl with you after I spotted Grim."

"Grim?" I reach for Tessa. Where Grim is, Antonio isn't far behind and he's about as deadly as they come.

Shaun nods, scanning the area around us like he can read my thoughts. "Grim led me on a goose chase. I couldn't get a shot and I couldn't blow up the pickup he had waiting for him either. The law is already going to be on top of us soon enough. So let's move. We need a new extraction point."

~

Tessa sweeps through the woods beside me just as silently as I taught her to. Shaun is ten yards ahead. He stops, crouching low under the summer shade of a wise old oak. I follow suit, Tessa doing the same, her fingers lacing through mine as we scan our surroundings. We're near the hardtop now, at least a mile downstream of Town's End. Not far enough for my liking but we had to move slowly.

Shaun motions us forward. "Be ready to move in ten."

Tessa looks at me and I nod. "You heard the man."

She gives my hand a squeeze and readies her feet. A van breaks around the curve a hundred yards away. "Now!" Shaun gives the order and we bolt from the woods. The back doors of the news van swings open. This is how the club has been blending in. They look like any of the other many news crews driving all over Hinton.

A second painted-up news van swings around the curve, back doors wide open. Shaun's arm flies backward and Tessa screams, his hand balling her shirt and hair into one tight fist. Panic surges through me. They're taking her.

"No!" I yell, my grip on Tessa's fingers failing. I can start shooting but they'll only shoot back.

Shaun hauls her to the first van, shoving her toward Rick, who is hanging out the back to receive his cargo. Her fingers claw at the edge of the door. "Warren!"

I slam into Shaun, his body blocking mine from hers. He spins around and throws an elbow into my jaw. I stumble left and run for the van speeding away from me. Tessa's face disappears behind Rick. He gives me a smile, and slams the doors closed. I let out a yell, taking my fury out on the bank beside me, firing bullets into the dirt. "She's mine!"

"She's *ours*." Shaun yanks my head back and Brian jumps out of the second van, ripping the gun from my hand and stripping the second from my holster. It's rare for me to feel the sting of tears but the club giving me a few blissful hours alone with Tessa, in a place where we felt safe, and then taking her from me... In all the life we've lived together, this is the one time I truly feel defeated.

Shaun lets go of me and Brian shoves me forward. I might be able to fend him off but I doubt I could even make it to the wood line before Shaun got a shot on me. Then there's Zeno sitting behind the wheel of the van I'm being forced into. I can go ahead and fight them all but it won't do any good. Tessa would still be gone and I'd be dead.

Power. That's what this is about. They're showing me they have dominance over me, and I'll be damned to hell before I let them give me this lesson. I shrug Brian off and climb into the back of the emptied-out shell of the van of my own accord. There's nothing inside here save for the two front seats. I move to the driver's side and press my back against the seat, lowering down and resting my hands on my bent knees. Shaun hops into the van, shutting the doors and giving the top a tap. Zeno spins off the road's shoulder, pinging gravel off the side of the van. I stare at Shaun and Brian. "Rick only found me because I was coming to find you. Let that sink in. Then tell Randy to return what's mine."

~20~

Tessa

I keep my eyes fixed on the men in the back of this van. Rick and Ian are returning my stare and I have no doubt that every time Randy checks his rearview he's giving me the same looks these two are. Despite everything else that's going on, my betrayals rank at the top of what they're angry about.

If the woman who planted a camera in their house had been Tina, Corrine, or any other female tight with the club, they would have let whatever man was closest to the girl deal with her. Maybe two wolves would have gotten involved. They sure as heck wouldn't have had the whole club prioritize hunting her down. Not even if her sister was a killer. I'm getting their special attention because I was as near to being one of them as a woman can be. Their guards were down with me. I didn't know where all their money came from but they trusted me to keep their books. Trust. The thing I broke that no one ever dreamed I would.

The van bumps over rough road, the jostling pulling a tear from my stinging eyes. Forasmuch as I love the men in front of me, now that I'm back in their possession, it all feels wrong. There's no Gary. No Chopper. And most of all, no Warren.

Rick's head cocks to the side. I've done a lot of crying this summer but the sight of my tears is still as foreign to him as the feel of them is to me. I rub my sweaty palm across my cheek. "If you kill Warren, you kill me."

He doesn't respond. Neither does Ian. They just look at me the same as they have been.

The van rolls to a stop. "Out," Randy orders from the front. I ease forward. Resisting will only make this worse for me and until I know Warren's fate, I'm not sure what it is I need to be fighting them for.

Ian throws the doors open and jumps out. Rick follows him, turning and holding a hand up to me. I want to hesitate but all that will get me is more distrust. I fit my palm in his and get out of this van a whole heap easier than how I got into it.

I look across the valley to the ridge I can see from here. The next one over is still smoking. We're not in Hinton anymore. Not technically anyway. But even this far out of town, we've been in this van longer than necessary. The club was doubling back, probably more than once, being sure our scent was covered while hauling down roads law enforcement doesn't have the manpower to cover.

Another news van rumbles down the dirt road. My breath catches. Rick tightens his hold on my hand so I wait. Anxious. Terrified. Thoughts racing to no place good.

The van parks beside ours and I stare at the back of it. The doors open and two wolves jump out, marching toward the cabin behind us. A tremor builds in my chest. I tug on Rick's hand and he lets go of me. I push my feet into gear and race for the van. Warren's head pops around the door, the sight of me drawing curses from his mouth. Happy ones. Words meant more as praise than blaspheme. I lock my arms around him and he plasters his around me. Randy stomps past us. "Inside. Now."

Warren loosens his arms and cups my face. "Stay behind me and stay close. If I can't hear you breathing, you're too far away."

"Ditto on the close and breathing part," I whisper, forcing the shake from my limbs and the tears from my eyes. "Don't let go of me and I won't let go of you."

He smiles. "It's about time."

~

Warren

Randy is on the porch of the small cabin, flanked by Shaun and Rick. Their van stunt was a point well made and if that's all it was, I'd be glad for it. But they meant it for a taste of what's to come. What Randy said to me at Town's End is true. The club will deal with Hinton's biggest problems and then they'll deal with the ones inside their own house.

A cool wind blows through the valley, swirling Tessa's hair over my shoulder. I look back to where her warm body is pressed up close to mine. "You feel that, baby? Summer will be over soon."

She smiles, a sad sentiment that doesn't register any hope of us living to see another season. "On the first day of fall, we'll find ourselves some greener pastures."

I nod. "I'm going to hold you to that promise."

Randy enters the cabin ahead of us, followed by Rick. We pass by Shaun and I resist the urge to punch him in the gut. He steps in behind us, closing the door and cutting off our exit. As if we'd chance running while all their eyes are on us.

I march us forward, walking in like I own the place. I stop in the center of the room and look around, taking note of who is gathered. More importantly, I take note of who isn't. Tessa's heart will never stop aching for the dead and I wish she didn't have to be at odds with the living.

I narrow my gaze on every wolf lining the walls, spinning slowly to make sure I don't miss one, including Bear. He's next to four others from Montrose's charter. I stay facing them as I speak my piece. "Anyone who wants to get to Tessa has to go through me, so if any of you feel like doing anything other than giving her an apology, step on up. Those are your two options. You can grovel at her feet or we can fight, but what you're not going to do is lay a finger on her. She's *mine*."

"And Warren is *mine*." She shoulders around me and stands at my side. "I haven't treated him like it in a long time but even when I was doing my best to hate everything about him, if I would have known that any of you were putting hands on him I would have stood up for him. But no one told me what was happening. I was kept in the dark and pushed aside." She looks straight at Randy. "How did that work out for you? From where I'm standing, nothing worked out for any of us. We failed each other and most of all, we failed Hinton."

This right here is what I love most about Tessa. The fierceness of her convictions. Even when she's wrong and doing stupid things like breaking up with me or storming city hall, she puts her all into it. It's why I'm so stuck on her. That boy inside me wants to follow her around just to see what the supernova is going to do next because when Tessa rides for you, dying seems impossible. It's not though, and right now we have as good of a chance as any of meeting our maker.

I tighten my grip around her waist. I wasn't stripped of my knife so that's either a sign that the club wants my hide now, or it's a sliver of respect. We'll find out soon enough. "Tessa and I have had some enlightening conversations. I was your errand boy, your punching bag, and Chopper's understudy. But I was never anything less to her than what I've always been. None of you will keep me from her again. Even if she demands it, *none of you will keep me from her again.* Understand?"

Shaun cracks his knuckles. "What we understand is that she betrayed us in our own house, and you ran off with her like you can steal what is *ours.*"

I jab a finger at him. "I took her because my *brothers* were failing to protect her. You scented and marked her, buying her boots and giving her rides all over town, but not one of you lived up to the promises Gary made me." I scan through the faces in front of us. "You didn't keep her safe. You let men and monsters alike put hands on her. You didn't step up when she needed you to so I did it for all of you." I rest my eyes on Randy. He's the one who bought her the riding boots, which is why I brought them up. "I swore an oath to this club and I meant every word, but I swore one to her long before that. Tessa is *mine.* Every one of you *will* keep your hands off her. And you're not holding a hair on her head accountable for anything because if you'd been doing your jobs, she wouldn't have been put into positions to betray you in the first place."

Brian shoves his arms over his chest. "She's responsible for her actions and we're responsible for ours. We'll *all* take our punishment for the wrongs we've done."

"Like hell we will," I growl. "If you want her, then you're fighting me and it's going to the death. If you feel like dying today, go right ahead and throw the first punch."

"No!" Tessa yelps. "Warren's a little high and he doesn't know what he's saying."

I dig my fingers into her side. "I'm just fine."

She waves her hands in a sign of peace, staving off the fight all of the men in this room are itching to have. Some because they mean it and others because we're frustrated with how our town and our lives are falling apart. "I wronged all of you, especially Chopper. He's dead because of me and before that I was the reason his actions crippled the club. Heap your hatred on my head because I deserve it. I won't be making excuses for myself, we're well beyond that and no amount of apologizing will make a bit of difference. But there's been enough death among us." She reaches around me and pulls herself in close. "As worried as Warren is about me, the only people he trusts to set the wrongs right are the men in this room. We have to stop fighting so we can take our town back. We need to find my sister. She's the next person to die."

Randy stomps across the floor, the hardness of the life he's lived written in the chiseled lines of his face. "The sister is going to die, because any threats we're aware of, we eliminate."

I snort. "That's the problem. I had to run off and lay low with my charge because the charter wasn't aware of any threats. You're all too relaxed in this sleepy town. But I'm wide awake and I told all of you that Matt Honaker needed to disappear. I got silenced. I won't be made to be quiet anymore. Tessa's crimes were done out of pure ignorance. Even the wall of hatred she built up against me can be chalked up to her bypassing her brain and jumping straight to conclusions. As bad as I want to punish her myself, I can't overlook her intentions and I'm not letting any of you forget them either."

Randy's hand shoves past Tessa and wedges under my chin, his fingers tightening around my throat. I don't fight him because that's not what this is. He's showing his place and I'm keeping mine. "We didn't know a lot of things. If we did, we would have handled the disobedience before now. Hers and yours."

"Good," I snarl. "I'm expecting more from this new leadership. I'm sure you're smart enough to understand that."

His eyes blaze. "The men in this room are *Leidolf*. Justice is what we *understand*, Gripr." He shoves my throat free, eyes hardening on Tessa. "We'll burn your sister to ash and you'll stand with us until it's done. After that, you'll stand and face your judgment just like the rest of us."

I drag Tessa from his stare, spinning her around and announcing one more thing the club will understand. I devour her mouth, kissing her in front of all of them because this says more than our words can. The atmosphere shifts around us and I smile against her lips. The way she kisses me isn't like what she did with Matt or even Chopper. This is heart and soul. All the proof they need that Tessa has *never* belonged to anyone but me. "Welcome home, baby. I bet these men can rustle us up a honeymoon suite."

The room we're shoved into isn't fit for a honeymoon but Tessa is still beside me so this too-small bed is just fine. I take a pill out of my pocket and chew it up. Now that I'm cut off from Dr. Lafferty I need to ration these. "You think Rick would call up his woman for me?"

Tessa plops against the headboard. "The club set off enough explosives to leave a section of road looking like the surface of the moon, so what I think is that you should learn to keep your mouth shut."

"You're one to talk," I mutter, tugging the satchel of pills from my pocket. I dump them into my palm, counting their dwindling numbers. "Showing the club weakness won't get their respect, Tessa. They're not going to grovel at our feet, but we're not falling on our knees in front of them either."

The door clicks open. Bear struts in and I let out a curse. He chuckles, tossing a first aid kit onto the bed. "And here I thought you'd be happy to get some fresh bandages. Both of you look like you could use some doctorin'. I'm happy to clean up the filly for you, Gripr."

I put the pills away and shove them back into my pocket. "To show my appreciation for your help with Dillon, and for you being kind enough to deliver these bandages, I'll tie one hand behind my back when I fight you to the point that your tongue is wrapped around your neck and your heart stops beating."

Bear's big arms cross over his chest, his tongue running over his teeth as he watches Tessa pop open the kit. "I might take you up on that fight one day, Gripr. I'd sure like to have myself one of her. What do you say, darlin'? You want to ride with the new head of the Northern Charter?"

I shove myself upward but Tessa falls across me. "Stop. He's baiting you and we've both already swallowed enough hooks."

Brian, Randy, and Zeno fill the doorway behind Bear. I set Tessa off me. "Yeah, we have. And it's time the rest of them do some swallowing because we're not the reason their reputations are soiled."

Bear clicks his meaty tongue. "It's a shame you and your li'l darlin' broke so many of our rules. I had high hopes for you." His eyes dart to Tessa and the corner of his lip ticks up. "I saw what you and Chopper did, Gripr." He levels back on me. "I was there the night you swept through a building and slaughtered my brothers. I didn't save them because I saw the tarnish, it started spreading out of Montrose the moment he turned his back on what the Leidolf stand for. I made my club a promise that night and I kept it. I might be sweet on your filly, but not at the expense of this club. I played my part before, and I did what needed doing. It's time you do the same. For us. Not her."

I get to my feet, fighting the urge to wrap an arm around my ribs. I stand up straight and look him square in the middle of his bushy-browed eyes. "Tessa first. Club second. Anyone who doesn't like it can bite me."

Brian groans. "He doesn't lack confidence, does he?"

Zeno chuckles. "Never has. Warren's been giving us hell since the day Tessa dumped him and it's been a heck of a lot of fun doling out his punishment."

Tessa lifts from the bed and stands next to me. "That's right, Zeno. Warren stood before all of you before he was ever one of you. Because he's not a coward. His only fault is the same one the rest of you have—misplaced loyalty to me. I'm a blight on all of your souls. A curse. So stop taking my sins out on Warren because there has never been a time when I wouldn't have laid down my life for any of yours. Not until right now. If any of you move against him you move against me. I love you and I *will* defend this club with my life, but my first loyalty is to Warren. I won't deny him anymore. Warren first. Club second. And I don't see why that's such a problem because there's nothing any of us don't agree on. Especially right now. Beth, and anyone helping her, dies."

Randy marches past Bear. "Your heart can belong to anyone you choose, Tessa, but *you* belong to *us*. Now get in the living room. Chief is holding a press conference." His eyes tear into me. "Keep running your mouth and I'll do what Gary ordered Chopper to do."

He turns and stomps back out of the room. I take hold of Tessa's hand and march us out behind him. Zeno falls in on my left, head ticking at the television. "This ought to be good."

I start to offer up another thing he'll like real good but Tessa clamps her nails into my skin. I return the gesture and focus on the television screen the same as everyone else, but my thoughts are trained on the woman whose nails are a heck of a lot sharper than mine. Her anger needs tempering or else she'll run off to be the martyr I have no intention of letting her be. I have to keep the Leidolf from separating us. The men care about her and most of them even love her, but they don't seem willing to stop reminding her of her wrongdoing. They'll let their words eat at her because they're arrogant enough to think they can stop her from doing whatever it is she wants to do. I choose to let her past actions inform my decision to keep my hands and eyes on her at all times.

The shot on the television pans to Chief. He's at city hall, on the same steps Tessa charged up after my warning for Matt to grab her went nowhere. Chief approaches the podium surrounded by officers. Durand is off to the side, scanning the crowd while Chief takes his position. From what the screen is showing when the cameras roam, not many townspeople are gathered, only news crews.

Chief clears his throat, the click of cameras nearly drowning out the sound. "Thank you all for coming today," he begins. "As has been reported, there was an incident early this morning involving Mayor Smith and his wife."

Tessa looks up at me. "His wife?"

Dread coils through my gut. "She must have known Chief is the one who did the shooting."

Tessa nods. "I bet she knew there were sex cameras in that room."

Randy looks at us. I shrug. "Our pious mayor shot porno as a side hustle and his wife knew. Tessa's probably right. There had to be cameras Chief didn't know about."

We turn our attention back to the screen and I can't help but feel sorry for the dead mayor's wife. Sorry that she was too preoccupied with her title and position to leave the man. It's one thing to walk your talk but when your strut doesn't match your words you're nothing but gutless. The woman knew her man was as two-faced as they come and she stayed with him until his bitter end sucked her down with him.

"I can't release the full details to you at this time," Chief continues his lie. "But during what was supposed to be a peaceful negotiation of surrender, members of the Leidolf biker club opened fire." He tugs on his collar, exposing the edge of a bandage that looks to be wrapped over his shoulder, another thick bandage around his wrist. "They shot me before I could keep them from shooting Mayor Smith."

None of us say a word. We might not have expected Chief to be brazen enough to go on television to call us out, but we already knew he was pinning the murder on the club. His hands cup the edges of the podium he's standing behind. "The residents of Hinton have been through a lot and they're being given few answers. They're afraid. And the more news coverage our once quiet town gets, the more rumors are spread. Let me ease your minds and calm your nerves. Every murderous member of the biker gang that infected our town will be brought to justice. To do this, law enforcement needs your cooperation." His eyes shift. To Durand. "As your police chief, I've come to a decision that some find unacceptable but we've tried imposing a curfew and it hasn't worked." He looks back out to the cameras. "Now, we're imposing our own form of martial law. Residents are to stay inside their homes. Open your doors for no one except law enforcement. Hinton is closed for business until we've rounded up all our trash. If you're harboring any, set it out on the curb. My men and I will be around to collect it soon."

He lets go of the podium but doesn't leave off laying down his new law. "Until this lockdown is lifted, anyone caught outside will be seeing the inside of a jail cell."

The reporters shout questions. Chief lifts his bandaged wrist, blocking the flashbulbs. "This is for your own good. Stay inside."

Chief's men fall in behind him and march down the steps. I draw myself closer to Tessa. "Are you getting it now? He never wanted to help you, he wanted to help himself. Now he's the judge, jury, and executioner. The first person he'll want to hold court for is you—the woman who knows too much."

~22~

Tessa

A cold chill is setting permanent gooseflesh over my body. I replay the news coverage in my mind and think back to Chief telling me that he couldn't get Mayor to leave his house. Chief had been wanting the mayor to stand in front of the news media to deliver the message he sent out today because he might not want tanks rolling down Main Street, but Chief wants control of this town. It wasn't Erin and Caleb dying like they did that set him to wanting the lockdown, they were only the catalyst to breaking him in a way that makes him think he's justified in writing laws with blood.

I fold my arms across my middle. Warren has me nestled into the crook of his arm but I don't feel any warmer. I hadn't even noticed Ian was missing until he called Randy just now. He's been in town at the press conference, being the club's eyes and ears.

Randy slams his phone down onto the dining table turned arsenal. "The strays were at the press conference. Ian clocked them. There are only four left but Ian couldn't get a clear shot. They were mixed into a group of reporters and he had to fall back when the law started cutting through the crowd. They're taking names, doing body searches, and arresting anyone who even has a pocket knife."

"That didn't take long," Warren huffs. "Chief wanted to bring his fist down on Hinton and he figured out how to do it so he'd have the support of his men."

I shake my head. "What about the state police and FBI? They're not going to let this happen."

Shaun grunts. "They'll do what suits them, and right now, letting the local lawman take over suits them."

Rick moves to the table where weapons are spread. "Too bad for them that Hinton belongs to us. It's ruled by our law, no one else's."

Randy rubs his jaw. "I'm going to make sure that's written in stone, but we're going to have to finish off the strays to do it. They capitalized on chaos in the aftermath of Chief's speech. Ian saw them grab two females. One is a reporter and he wasn't sure about the other."

I swallow. "They're taking hostages?"

Warren leads us to the table the others are gathering around, clicks filling the air around us. But unlike what we heard on the news, these clicks are from guns, not cameras. "They're dead men walking, baby. They're not interested in hostages."

"Vengeance." I choke on the word. "I guess we're fixing to find out who wants it more."

Zeno tugs one of his throwing knives from a slot on his belt and presses it into my palm. "Just like your sister's victims, no one the strays touch will survive. If they get near you, use this blade the way Chopper taught you."

I nod, holding back tears Chopper wouldn't be happy to see. "I'll make him proud. I'll make all of you proud."

"You will not," Warren grumbles, taking the blade and shoving it back at Zeno. "She's already done her part and I already told all of you that no one is getting to her because no one is getting by *me*. Now keep your weapons to yourself because you're lucky she didn't already slice her fingers off with that."

The men in the room chuckle. Warren narrows his eyes at me. "They're laughing because they all know it's true. My old lady is a walking hazard. One who's going to keep herself glued to my side because you owe me a wedding and I intend to get it."

Randy leans his palms on the table. "We're all owed many things. It's time to collect. Time to take back all that belongs to us because we will not cede control to anyone. Not the strays, and not the law. This town belongs to *us*. No one stands against us, so let's clean our house and bury our dead."

I pivot away from Warren so I don't have to see him be disappointed in me. I stare only at Randy. "Put me in, Coach, because no one does vengeance better than me and I know how to end all of this."

~

Beth

I turn the television up. I almost missed the press conference because of Gena's sniveling. I tried telling her that she wouldn't have to moan around like that if she had a normal table with a square edge instead of this stupid oval-shaped table with no edges at all. It's the same kind Tessa has. Seeing it in Gena's kitchen was enough of a reason for me to pick up the bat the paranoid old woman greeted me with at the door. Her having the nerve to set cookies out of a box onto a platter, like if she presented them that way it would hide her laziness, is why I hit her the second time.

"Shut up," I blare. Somehow her moaning is getting louder. Like everyone else in this town, she's worried about herself instead of bothering to think about what I'm going through. If Arnold had met me back in town like I asked him to, I wouldn't waste my time killing her. I'd let him do it. She's not his type, anything with pubic hair isn't, but he's long overdue in repaying me for all that I've done for him. I stand overtop Gena. "Arnold is worse than you. I gave him the time of his life and where is he now? Nowhere." I ram the tip of my shoe into her cheek. "He couldn't be bothered to do the one simple thing I asked of him because he's as ungrateful as Tessa."

Gena's lips part, some kind of gross noise blubbering out through all the slobber. I swing the bat over my head and bring it down on her teeth. "I said, shut up!"

She stops moving. Finally. I toss the bat aside, that platter of cookies drawing my eye. I wipe the blood off the edge of one. Gena stood right here complaining about her twin nephews all while never once apologizing for not bothering to make me a fresh batch of anything. She brought a pan of brownies into the post office for Marla just three weeks ago so I know it wouldn't have been too much for her. I crunch down on the hard exterior of the gingersnap. "Maybe if you'd been more thoughtful, you wouldn't be toothless right now." I drop the cookie onto her chest. "They're stale."

I go back to the television mounted underneath her cabinets. I had high hopes for this press conference. It should have been my moment. The time when I was named, the mayor himself quivering his lips over the lives I've taken while every reporter blasted the details on their own stations, hailing me as the best killer to ever grace their channels. Instead, the mayor went and got himself killed and Chief Dunbar didn't breathe a word about any death outside of that one. Tessa and her biker gang robbed me again. And she had the nerve to do this to me after not showing up at Mom's house. I had the cameras all set up. Nanny cams placed just right so I could see Tessa's face when she found all the little presents I left for her. And the sound... I was planning on a good night's sleep with the sound of Tessa's screams for my lullaby.

I flip through the news channels. There's not even a peep about Erin and that bastard son of hers. *"Are the Leidolf responsible for the explosions that rocked Hinton earlier today?"* I mock the reporter. *"More importantly, why did they assassinate Mayor Smith? Something sinister is happening in Hinton.* Yeah, moron, *I'm* happening. Me! Who cares about the mayor and this so-called reporter that went missing?" I lean toward the screen. "Me. I matter! I. Matter."

The news coverage flashes to a perimeter that was set up around Town's End, Warren's sign bright and shiny on the screen for everyone to see. I rip the television from the brackets and sling it. He's rubbed himself in my face for the last time.

I pace to the window and pull the corner of the curtain back. The houses around Gena's are all dark. There's been a steady flow of traffic on the street ever since Chief made the announcement for everyone to stay put. People aren't listening to him. They're fleeing, leaving their houses empty. I think I'll go by the Bridgewaters'. They have a big jetted tub and the refrigerator was always well stocked when I used to babysit their girls. Maybe I'll get lucky and they'll still be home. Nolan always did remind me of Warren. I had vivid fantasies of him and just like Warren, he denied having them about me. He hired someone else to babysit and would act like he hardly knew me when I'd see him in town. If he's home, he's going to know me tonight.

I drop the curtain. A quadruple murder is just what I need. That'll get these news people to focus on what's important. Warren can hide Tessa but he can't keep me from her. Wherever she's at, she's going to see me on every channel, and I'm going to close my eyes and imagine her screaming just the way she did for Gary.

"Gena?" I make my way back to her. She slides an arm out to the side, her elbow smearing right through the blood pooling around her. Finally something good is coming my way. This is always better when they're still alive. I kneel beside her. "Have you ever held a human heart?"

~23~

Tessa

A storm is coming. Not a light summer rain to drizzle away the humidity but a raging tempest meant to turn creeks into rivers. Floods will flash just as surely as the lightning is painting the distant sky. It's still a way off though, and I can only hope we finish this before the rains come. Tonight, the Leidolf fight for Hinton. Before dawn shines again the club will have the names of any man or woman who has touched a child and they'll mete out that justice. Bear's remnant charter will put down the strays. The law will know its place. And if Beth hasn't come to me before then, I'll go to her.

I lift my face to the swirl of the storm's warning, hair tickling over my shoulders and slapping back across my cheeks. Warren runs his fingers through the tangled strands, twirling the frizzy mess into his fist. He's angry, but he's with me, standing in the shadow of a boxcar waiting for the others to signal us. He thinks my plan is too risky and it is. I tried to convince him and the others to let me do this part alone but none of them were willing to agree. The fact that I even tried to make a case for this being a solo mission infuriated Warren. Unlike the last couple of days, he's been silent since we left the cabin.

A light flashes twice in the distance, taking a short pause before flashing once more. It isn't lightning. It's Rick and Zeno signaling that the wolves are in place. The strays and Beth are all looking for me so I'm going to let them find me, and while I'm doing that, the club will keep tanks from rolling down our streets. They've already reached out to their contacts, whether they be in law or politics and whether those connections are mutual or coerced. We don't want more casualties in this war, we want every kill tonight to be justified.

"It's time," Randy affirms from beside us. "Stick to the plan, Gripr. Run from us again and you die."

Warren's fist tightens in my hair, his body pressed close against my back. I rest a hand on Randy's arm, soothing his nerves since Warren isn't. "Nothing will ever be what it used to, we've all lost too much. But I never intended to hurt the club. Take my word for the little it's worth to you right now, but in my heart, I'm as much of a wolf as any of you. I just lost my way when I broke up with Warren. And now I've lived all the days without him that I'm willing to. We're not running. We're standing with the club because what I am in my heart, Warren fully is. He's Leidolf."

Randy eyes us. "We never doubted that either of your hearts belonged to each other but we never guessed you'd break your loyalties to us. So hear me. Loyalty is what we're owed and it's what we're going to get. Remember that tonight. We *all* right our wrongs."

His footsteps are too silent to hear as he moves away. A smile tugs its way onto my lips. So many of these men are of few words but they've been forced to speak lately, and hearing their voices is comforting.

Randy's shadow disappears and Warren blows out a breath. "Well, aren't you just downright happy now? You've wiggled your way right back into the center of everything I've been trying to get you out of."

I tug my head, trying to free my hair of his grip. "Remind me of when I wasn't in the middle of it. I seem to have forgotten that part."

He lets go of my hair and turns me to face him. "This plan of yours is wrong and you know it. We've already survived one fire and you're putting us right back into another one."

His words ring true and my gut pinches because there are other truths at play here and they're all bigger than me standing inside my own house while fire licks up the sides of it. I press my palms to the roughness of his jaws. "You don't have to do this with me. I can rig the stove on my own. I'll start the fire by myself and I promise you I'll get out in time. I *promise* I will come back to you. The only thing I won't promise is that I'll stay hiding away while our town continues to die. It isn't only Beth and the strays anymore. You saw the cars in the street. Half of them were empty because Chief is rounding people up and storing them in the Wiggly Pig. That's not right, Warren."

He rests his forehead on mine. "No, it isn't. But there's no law saying you're the one who has to fix it. You didn't tell your buddy to lose his mind and you're not one of the men out there following his orders to lock people in a grocery store. You didn't turn Beth into a psychopath and you didn't make the strays shrug off the skin they were hiding in. They're not even playing at being wolves anymore, Tessa. Whether your plan to draw them out works or not, you're narrowing the eye of this storm right down to the very center of your chest."

"Which is only a problem for you." I dig my fingers into his growing scruff. Before long, he really will look like a wolf. One who is wild and free. "I love you, Warren, and I know you love me just as much. We're as right for each other as we are wrong and I meant what I just told Randy, so don't twist what I'm getting ready to say."

I open my mouth to finish my thoughts. To ask him again to run. To go to Marcie. I'd pay people to commit to a lie that he lost his life in the housefire and I'd make them take the truth of his ghost to their graves. But Warren isn't interested in hearing what I have to say. He closes his mouth over mine, the kiss deep, angry, and just as forceful as it is sweet.

He lets go of my lips but holds me in place with an iron grip. "I've seen this look in your eye plenty enough, so you're the one who needs to stop twisting words. You getting hurt tonight is going to be one heck of a problem for a lot more people than only me. I'll fight with the club and I'll even rise up to be their new Chopper. I'll be the cleanest, meanest killer they have. But if you get hurt tonight, it's going to be *them* I kill. Randy should have never agreed to using you as bait."

I smooth my hands over Warren's shoulder. "If I get hurt tonight, that only means you won't be forced to live under lock and key because you know as well as I do that when this war is over, the club is going to lock me down. They're going to keep us separated for a long time, make us prove our loyalty by staying away from one another, and you can make that process so much easier by choosing Marcie. You didn't hurt the club like I did. They'll end your punishment sooner than mine and it will happen all the faster if you don't fight for me. Just be with Marcie. You can even marry her if you want because *nothing* will break us."

"Except you," he spits. "The club can help me guard what's mine but I won't be handing you over to them again. They already had their chance with you and they're not exactly giving me a gut full of confidence that they've learned their lesson, seeing how you're practically off on a suicide mission right now."

I drop my hand to the hem of his sleeve, the bandage I applied to the worst of his burns poking out beneath the black material. "One wolf nearly killed you, Warren. *One*. Don't make me watch the others take turns beating you because you know they will. *You* are the punishment they will break me with."

~

I've always heard that to be famous, your name needs to be painted in lights. I'm going to do the television people one better. Tonight, my face will shine with the blaze of a thousand flames. If I do this fire right, they'll get the shot of me standing in the front window while the house around me burns. Beth will see it. The strays. And I predict they'll all come running. If I'm dead they'll want proof and if I'm alive they'll want to get their hands on me, if only to make sure I finally do stop breathing.

I tried again to convince Warren that my plan is a good one when he was dragging me through the train yard. His grip on my hand only got worse. He's not keeping me from doing this though. He stayed glued to me as I walked myself through town, avoiding the law but little else. I wanted as many eyes to see me as possible and I'm certain Warren and I made some cameos in the news footage being continually broadcast from inside our small town.

"I don't know why you're being so sour about this, Warren. You're the one who wanted to burn my house down to begin with."

He covers his nose, the stench inside my house not a pleasant one. The bodies are gone but the place hasn't been cleaned. "You're right, Tessa, but I wasn't going to burn it down with you in it."

I move away from him, taking in the home I spent very little of my time in. Someone, probably the law, pillaged through my personal belongings looking for whatever they could find. Too bad for them that as close as I was to the club, I didn't know their secrets. The little I was privileged with wouldn't have been enough to hurt the club even if I'd kept a diary and written it all down.

I walk into what was my bedroom and pick up the overturned picture frame on my dresser. It's a photograph that Cheryl gave me, of her bright smiling face puckered up beside Gary's shoulder. His grin is as wide as the row of candles on the cake he's holding. This is from Gary's last birthday. Cheryl came to sing for him and I remember the exact moment when she took this picture. Now she doesn't get to sing anymore and Gary can't celebrate another birthday, all because of Beth.

I flip the frame back over and open it, sliding the photograph out. I slip it into my back pocket, jumping when Warren barks. "The stove is rigged. Get what you need and then get out. This old bedroom of yours is going to be ash soon."

He checks the gas valve on the old wall heater that I was always too scared to use. I lift the top of my grandmother's old jewelry box. Someone broke the hinges. The rusty metal used to stick, so you had to open it just right.

Whoever wanted inside this box didn't know you had to be sweet to the hinges. "We're only supposed to torch the place, Warren, not blow it up."

He rips a bottle of fingernail polish remover out of an open drawer and starts dousing the walls. "You got to walk up the middle of the road flaunting yourself for everyone to see, I get to bring these walls down any way I like."

I take Samantha's gold chain from the box. Whoever broke into Grandma's scratched-up keepsake was disappointed to see that everything inside it was fake. I clip the chain around my neck and tuck the sparkly unicorn pendant underneath my shirt. "You do remember the part of the plan where we're supposed to actually make it out alive, right?"

Warren stomps up behind me. "You wanted to be a spectacle, so I'm making sure you're a darn good one, sweetheart. What are you over here dragging your feet about? We need to move."

I lift the string of plastic beads he gave me from the bottom of the box. "There are few things inside this house that mean anything to me, and this is the only one I can't live without."

He snatches the fake pearls away, shaking them between us. "We're fixing to die in this housefire over some cheap junk I gave you?"

I reach for the beads and he yanks them away, a grin spreading over his face. "Well, aren't you just a sweet thing? I guess I don't need Marcie after all." I punch him in the gut and he chuckles, tugging my fisted hand forward and twining the pearls around my wrist. "Baby, I'll buy you the real thing and you can wear them on our wedding day. Now move your sweet little tail."

He pulls me out of the room and down the hall. This fire will draw law and news alike, serving as the distraction the Leidolf needs. It's also my chance to snatch a reporter of my own. Chief had the right idea when he went on television to deliver a message. I have one for Beth to hear.

We reach the kitchen, gas from the stove already strong in here. I tug on Warren's hand. "I'm supposed to stay long enough to be seen in here."

"Too late for that," he grumbles, heading for the door. It kicks open, the frame filling with the one face I wasn't hoping to see tonight.

My heart falls through the floor beneath me. "Chief, I wouldn't shoot that gun if I were you."

He trains his barrel on Warren. "I'm going to enjoy this. It's what I should have done the day you were born."

~24~

Beth

I saw this in a movie once, a family found dead around their dining room table. I thought the theatrics of the whole thing was as lame then as I do now. I prefer the shock that comes with people being found turned inside out. Matt liked it too. He got off on every little gasp made after a body was found. People just couldn't stop talking about the horror of it. I learned that after Layla died. I mostly cut her up to hide her identity, keeping only the parts I took out of her while she was still alive. It wasn't much. She didn't like my knife inside her as much as she liked having a boy inside of her. I told everyone that she was sleeping with all the men in town but that only made them want her more. They looked at her like she was the choicest cut of beef.

After she was gone, I regretted having concealed her identity. I should have fileted Layla and dropped her body in the street for all of those drooling boys to cry over. It wasn't enough for me to start a rumor that the body had been hers, most of them chose to believe it wasn't because they preferred to hope she'd be back one day. It was only the women in town who gasped and gossiped. I didn't even manage to get Gary jailed for the murder. He and Tessa just kept right on living their perfect little lives.

I pull Nolan's head back and run my blade down the sweaty plane of his neck, careful not to nick the bag over his head. Every death since Layla's has served a deeper purpose, and while this particular scene is doing nothing for me personally, it's necessary. Besides, Nolan deserves to die. He didn't even put up a fight. To get him into his place at the head of the table, all I had to do was sneak into the girls' room and convince them to come downstairs with me. I even got a bonus child, the neighbor's little girl spending the night.

These kids thought it was a game. A trick we were going to have fun playing. When they saw the dog from the backyard opened up on top of the dining room table they got scared. I told the little brats that if they screamed, they'd be carved up like the mutt in front of them. They quieted down. I zip-tied them to their chairs with ties that came from Nolan's own garage and then told them to scream. Nolan came running. When he saw me, he had the nerve to call me crazy.

"That's good, Daddy." I breathe deeply, showing him how. "Keep your eyes on Mommy. It's her turn."

I move toward his wife. He bucks his restraints but that only sucks away his oxygen faster. He moans, a pathetic sound. The girls wail, screaming for him. I slam my hand against the table. "Quiet!" They stifle their wailing but I can still hear their whimpers. I yank their mother's head from the table.

I had to use my taser on her because unlike her husband, she was going to fight me.

The overhead lights dim, the crystals hanging from the gaudy chandelier shaking. The boom comes next. Not one that's caused by the storm breaking open the sky. I race to the front of the house. Sirens echo down the street, the blares all heading in the same direction. They're racing to where dark clouds are being lit by the glow of a fire. "No!" I scream, hurrying to the television and flipping through the channels. This is supposed to be my night. I'm going to kill this family and tip off the news. They'll bring their cameras here and then I'll finally get what I was always meant to have. *I'm what's important.*

I stare at the screen. My sister's house is engulfed in flames behind the reporter whose umbrella is failing to keep the rain off his head. "This home right here behind me is one connected to the Leidolf bike club. It was the scene of what police called at the time *a gang shooting.* We were on location when they recovered the bodies involved in that crime and..." He turns to the side, nodding along with whatever the short, dark-haired woman is whispering in his ear.

"What?" I hit the television. "Tell me!"

A box pops up in the corner, footage of Tessa and Warren walking hand in hand playing right in front of me as the reporter continues. "It's now confirmed that the couple filmed walking through town together earlier tonight were spotted going inside this burning home. It appears they went in through the front door and only a handful of minutes later, an explosion tore through not only the front that you can see now, but another and *larger* explosion ripped through the back of this small house." He pauses. "Retaliation. Retribution. We don't know what happened here tonight but we do know that no one is expected to have survived. I'm Paul West.

Stay with me as I continue to bring you breaking news from right here inside Hinton."

"No!" I hit the screen. "No, no, no!" I shove the television from the entertainment center and stomp back into the dining room. "Do you see now? Huh? Do you see why I have to do this?" I scream at Nolan. He's already dead. I don't even get to feel the warmth of his blood take its last pump through his heart. Tessa has robbed me of every joy.

I turn to the brats who just won't stop crying. Their faces are all splotchy and red. Now the video I was going to make of me killing them won't be as powerful. They're not cute anymore, they're just snotty little kids. I lift my knife over the oldest one's head, a chill sweeping up my arms. I lower the blade and look around. The hair on the back of my neck stands up and I run for the door. I'm not sticking around to see if my intuition is right. I'd rather be wrong about not being alone in the house anymore than dead.

I throw open the door and race down the front steps. Thunder rolls across the sky and the rain falls even harder, matching the frantic beat of my heart as I run. A police car turns onto the street, flashing his lights at me. I tuck my knife behind my back and head for the lights, waving my free hand as if I'm relieved to see the law. The officer pulls to the side, opening the door and walking toward me. "Ma'am, I'm going to need you to stop right there."

I keep running. "He has a gun!"

The officer looks over my shoulder, scanning the thick sheets of rain. "Who?"

"You," I laugh, plunging my knife into his neck. I rip the blade out and throw my weight into him, taking the gun he's so graciously unholstering for me. I shove him to the side. He falls onto the wet pavement, gasping, his blood mixing with rain and washing away before I even get to enjoy it. This whole night has been a waste. Because of Tessa.

I drop into the dying man's seat and toss his gun into the floorboard, slamming the door and resting my knife in my lap. There's water everywhere. I wipe the rain out of my eyes and put the car in gear, driving down the road in the direction I just ran from, watching the shadows, squinting to see through the dark and the rain. Right out in the open, standing in the lit-up front doorway of the Bridgewater home, is Zeno. There's a gun in his right hand and a phone in his left. I blow him a kiss he can't see and hit the gas. "Nice try, gang boy. Big sister is smarter than the dummy who just got herself roasted. Stew on that while I go make sure she's dead."

~25~

Warren

I told Tessa this plan of hers was a bad idea. Parading around town before rigging her house to go up in flames was never *not* going to be a trap. I can't say I expected it to be Chief who showed up, I didn't even expect Beth. That's why I wanted us out of that house before it ever went up in smoke. If the strays came for us, we wouldn't be living to tell the tale to this news crew Tessa wrangled up. Paul West and his people being on scene from the first spark is the only part of this bright idea that's panned out the way she wanted it to.

"Darn you, Tessa," I growl, applying as much pressure to her bleeding shoulder as I can. Even prepared for her to do something stupid, it still happened too fast for me to do anything about it. She jumped in front of a bullet meant for me. "You're lucky Chief only hit you in the shoulder."

Her eyes flutter. "Did he make it out?"

"I hope not," I squawk at her. Chief's bullet made such a clean pass that I can't believe he didn't get two river rats with one bullet. The instant I felt her move it seemed like I was on her, heaving us forward, right through Chief and out the door, heat and flames licking over my skin. My shirt caught fire. I held onto her and pushed until grass was underneath us and sky was above us. It broke open, greeting our arrival with a thunderous roar. I rolled, the water helping to douse my flames. Then the second blast answered the storm, spewing burning debris up to meet the rain. I curled my body around hers. If it hadn't been for Paul West's cameraman being so determined to get his money shot, I'm not sure we would have made it.

My head sags. The blood pumping out of Tessa isn't only from her shot-up shoulder. Her swollen face is trickling with it, cuts and splits bleeding as bad as my own. The back of the news van opens and Paul West himself crawls inside, soaking wet, just like Tess and me. "It's done. The fire trucks are rolling in and that Bobby fella went on record confirming your identities. The rest of the crew is out catching everything they can on film." He nods to where Tessa is bleeding all over their floor. "Are we taking her to the hospital now?"

"No," she moans, clenching her teeth and squirming underneath my palms. "Now would be a good time for Warren to share his pocket full of pills with me though. If Beth is coming, she'll be coming soon."

I nudge my hip toward Paul. My hands are too bloody to feed her the drugs she needs. "Bear and his ragtag charter are out there, baby. They'll take care of Beth if she comes."

"No," Tessa wheezes. "They're here for the strays. Beth is mine."

I growl at her. "You've already played right into Beth's hands enough, I'm not letting you do it again."

Tessa's wide-set eyes blaze, no regard for the blood soaking down over her arm. "If Beth is here, she dies by my hand."

"Good," I snarl, sarcasm so thick it's choking. "Because you got yourself shot so all you have is *one* hand."

Paul slowly lifts the flap on my pocket and pulls out the satchel. "I still get the exclusive, right? No matter what happens, you two are sticking with me and giving me the interview so I can lay this whole story out on the news tomorrow? Favorably, of course."

I feel the vein in my neck throbbing, my muscles so tight they're liable to snap from my bones. "Feed this woman those pills and shut the hell up before I lay *you* out. Favorably, of course."

"Warren," Tessa pants. "He's not the enemy. We'll give him what he's owed but not at the expense of missing Beth. Check with Bear. Make sure he knows to take her alive. That kill is mine, even if both my arms get shot off."

Tessa's eyes roll back in her head. I lean over her. "Nothing is yours until we get these holes in you patched up so open your freaking eyes, baby. Paul here is going to go fetch us a sewing kit and then I'm going to repay the fine stitching you did on my head."

~

The only thing worse than knowing Tessa would drag herself after Beth with holes in both her shoulders and her feet cut off is knowing she wouldn't be doing it out of hatred. She'd be doing it for love. Just like she stayed on her feet while she stitched me up because of the love we've shared. I wish I could have done that for her but when Paul's dark-haired producer brought me that little sewing kit, I chickened out. I couldn't thread that needle through her skin. I used their first aid kit to bandage the front of her shoulder and then called for Bear.

I hold Tessa tight, her legs wrapped around my waist and her bare chest pressed against mine. "Almost done, baby," I whisper against her ear, the smell of her singed hair filling my nose. Her fingernails have drawn blood from my back a time or two, but she's drugged up good now so she's barely moved. The news van did, though. I had West relocate us down the street from all the commotion in case Tessa went to screaming. I should have known she wouldn't.

Bear sews up the last jagged edge of skin on her back. Her legs tighten around me when he pulls the needle through, her mouth pressed hard against my shoulder. I fan my fingers over the small of her back. "You're doing good, Tess. So darn good."

Bear is as impressed with her as I am. I can see it in the gleam of his eye. He ties off the thread and grins at me. "Now that we've kicked this can over and you've let me see her naked, what else am I gonna get to do with your filly?"

I motion to his chest. "You get to hand her your shirt. Mine's a little charred."

She takes a shallow breath, lips grazing the side of my neck. "If you'd stop cutting my clothes off me, I'd have my own to wear. You owe me two shirts and a string of wedding pearls, Gripr."

Bear eyes the plastic beads on her wrist, the cheap things somehow surviving the shower we took in burning debris. He peels his shirt off. "It really is a cryin' shame the sister isn't a twin."

I slip his shirt over Tessa's head. "You'll have to settle for just letting my woman star in your dreams. This visual right here should help. I know I like it when she's in my clothes."

He grunts, dour but approving. I curl a hand through Tessa's hair and hold the other out to him. If Bear hadn't been here to step in, I was on the verge of driving her to the hospital. With the current state of our crazed lawmen, that likely wouldn't have worked out for us. "Thank you, brother. I appreciate everything you've done for us. I won't forget my debt to you."

He takes my offered hand, giving it a firm shake before letting go and crossing the logs he calls arms over his now bare chest. "No debts, Gripr. We're even. If not for you helping to save my charter the night you came with Chopper, I wouldn't still have men left who can call themselves Leidolf. We ride with the Hinton Charter until our strays are put down, and then we ride for home."

His eyes scan over Tessa and I run my hands along the legs she has wrapped around my waist. "You might want to get started on leaving because that leer of yours is going to put us right back to not being friends."

His tongue flicks over his lips. "I'll be gettin' soon enough. The road to rebuilding the Northern Charter is going to be about as long as the one Hinton's going to have to ride before order is fully restored."

"We'll have the support of the town by morning," Tessa mutters from my shoulder. "That's why I got us our own personal news crew. They're going to tell our story *our* way."

"Maybe so," Bear answers her, his eyes glued to mine. "I don't know what's going to be left of you and your filly in the end, but the two of you will always be welcome in the north. It would be an honor to have you ride with me because one of her isn't the only thing I could use. If Hinton gets too stuffy for you, come to me."

I put my eyes on this woman in my arms. "Hinton's just now starting to be a place I can call home again."

Bear sighs. "I figured as much but the offer stands, Gripr. Now feed her a couple more of those pills. The strays are on the move, and the sister was spotted."

~26~

The roar of the storm beating down on the top of this van is doing little to drown out my thoughts. One different decision made on my part and none of us would be sitting outside the Bridgewater home, huddled in the back of an overcrowded news van with Zeno filling us in on how he made the call to help the little girls inside the house rather than chase Beth.

He made the right call, tending to the children and their mother until he heard the ambulance arriving. He just shouldn't ever have been put in a position to make that decision to begin with. If I'd just said no to that job Jessop painted up like it was the down payment on all of my dreams, all of our lives would be different. Instead, that gussied-up lie ended my relationship with Tessa and led everyone in Hinton right into the middle of Armageddon.

I tighten my fingers through Tessa's. She wouldn't have holes in both sides of her shoulder if I'd poured myself down on her, told her I was thinking about doing a fake robbery because I was too prideful to let her be the one paying for the house we planned on moving into. She would have corrected my thinking and that would have staved off her family's ability to tear down what I always made a point of building up. Then Beth couldn't have spent these years living under Tessa's roof, manipulating everyone in town, and getting herself overlooked by the club.

Maybe not having unfettered access to Tessa would have made Beth come unglued sooner. Or maybe she would have never escalated into the straight-out-of-hell demon she is today. Either way, she'd still be a killer. One the club would have caught by now because if I'd been a man instead of a boy, Tessa would never have been so embedded with the club. She would have been in my bed, and whether I turned Leidolf or not, I would have made sure they didn't parade her around town like their dang mascot. They made it clear to everyone that she was special among them, and that's what got Montrose and his men salivating to get their hands on her. Once that threat to her was made, Gary and the others were preoccupied with thinking all of the murders were connected to enemies moving against them instead of looking right under their noses.

The back of the van opens, rainwater pouring inside as Paul West and his cameraman clamber to get out of the storm. Their rain gear is pointless in this weather. Even Randy and Rick were soaked to the bone by the time they made it from their little sedan into the van.

"The officer who was stabbed is dead," West reports, water running off his clothes to pool on the floor where Tessa's blood is still staining everything pink. "He bled out before the ambulance got here but his car was just found abandoned." His eyes land on Tessa. "Three streets away from the house fire."

She inhales sharply, pressing a soothing hand to her shoulder. "Beth came. I told all of you that she would."

A pain shoots behind my left eye, this headache building faster than the tension in this van. For Beth to risk showing up at the house means she's crazed to the point of being willing to do *anything* to get her hands on Tessa. While I was off licking my wounds and pretending I'm not just as jealous and stubborn as Tessa, Beth got comfortable with the torture she was able to inflict. Now she's missing being able to watch Tessa suffer and there's no telling what her sick little brain is going to convince her to do next.

"The girls and their mom?" I ask, only because I know this news will be better than what we've heard so far.

West's eyes dart to Zeno and then back to mine. "The kids told the police that a scary man chased away the bad woman. The oldest child named Beth as the bad woman, but the police are making statements saying that Beth is a known associate of the Leidolf."

Rick rests his elbows on his knees. "What statements are you making?"

West swallows. "I'm reporting the truth as I know it. Mr. Bridgewater was murdered by Beth. The girls, their mother, and their friend were all tortured by Beth, with a yet unidentified man saving them. You all tell me when and how you want yourselves identified, and I'll break the story." He scans Zeno's face again. "I'd love an interview with you."

"No," Zeno answers, thickening the tension to smothering levels.

West runs a hand through his wet hair. "Emergency crews pulled off subduing the house fire. They say that with the rain, it's contained enough to not spread to any nearby houses."

As if confirming the truth of his words, the rain picks up, thundering down like a stampede of wild horses. Tessa sits forward. "The Wiggly Pig. This whole town is about to flood and that store is ground zero. The creek on the far side of the parking lot overflows its banks in lesser storms than this one."

Randy pulls out his phone and dials who I assume is Shaun, seeing how Shaun was sent to keep an eye on the pigs holding townspeople hostage in the supermarket. "Get ready. We're on our way. If the law tries to stop us from getting those people out, we go hot."

Randy hangs up and nods to Rick. Rick reaches over his shoulder and taps on the driver's seat where West's producer is doing her best to eavesdrop. "Move. I'm driving."

The woman scrambles into the passenger seat and West shuffles forward, anxious energy vibrating around him. "Will you be using the explosives you used before?"

Randy gives him a blank stare. Zeno plucks a knife from his belt and begins to clean his fingernails. "What explosives?"

West watches the knife, his face paling and his jaw working as he moves into a seat against the wall. "I forgot the Leidolf weren't involved in what happened. My mistake." He opens his mouth again but his cameraman shakes his head, telling West to stop talking. Good advice.

The van moves down the street and I curl Tessa against me. Her idea to have our own personal reporter is only a good one if West doesn't report the wrong thing, and he's hankering for an exclusive that will make his career. Us going against the police isn't the kind of juicy story we need to feed him. He needs to report this for what it is, the police turning on our whole town. "After we rescue people from the Wiggly Pig, we can house some of them at Town's End. It's well above the floodplain. Even my house is."

Randy narrows his eyes on me. "Any rescue who can't go back to their own house can go to the Grille. You can go with them, and make yourself useful in the kitchen."

I meet his glare with one of my own. "I'm not much of a cook but I can sure go to the Grille and pack up Tessa's closet. She won't be needing a room there anymore. I got a real nice one for her at my place."

Randy leans forward. "Gripr, everything you have belongs to the club. *Everything.* Part of it we loaned you the money for and the other part got shot on your watch."

I mimic his posture. He's not going to do to me what Gary did. I'm not getting kicked out of Tessa's life again, fed lies, and made to grapple for scraps. Gary used our split as a means to control me. He kept me separated from her because he knew I'd do anything to get close to Tessa again and he saw that as an opportunity to get me to do his bidding. Which I did, while also taking beatings and promises that he wouldn't let any other man get to her before I had my chance to settle my peace with her. That was a lie from the first moment Gary made me the promise. I'll not be walking that road again.

"You're about half right, *Coach.* I do owe the club money. I'll repay every dime of that loan Gary gave me and I won't even deduct what *I'm* owed for services rendered. But this hole running through Tessa's shoulder is *your* fault. So you just let me know when you're ready to settle up. I'm good for payment whenever you are."

Randy's steely eyes don't leave mine. "This daughter of the Leidolf says we finish this by dawn. You can pay me by dusk."

~27~

The resentment between Randy and me is growing. He's showing dominance and I'm not cowing to it. I could, and I will, whenever the decisions he makes are the right ones. I shift how Tessa is sitting on my lap. We're in the front of the van now, keeping watch over the Wiggly Pig from across the street. Randy and the others are on the opposite side of the store with the arsenal Shaun dug up. Once the charter is gathered, they'll give the law one chance to be on their side before taking the people out of the aisles of that doomed store by force. According to Shaun, there are forty people inside the Wiggly Pig and only five of them are cops.

My job in all of this is to guard the reporter. He's vital to making sure Hinton gets back on the side of the Leidolf. So when Randy told me to keep the people in this van far enough away from the action to not be in the middle of it, but close enough for them to get the scoop the club wants them to have, I wasn't arguing. West and his crew are Tessa's brainchild so she can make sure the people in the back don't do anything the club wouldn't approve of while I make sure *she* doesn't do anything *I* don't approve of. She won't admit it, but she's in no shape to even be sitting in the front of this van with my arms around her.

I rub her back, well below the gunshot wound. The pills are good at soothing pain but they only help for a little while, and Tessa's better than me, she doesn't want to take more than what I already fed her. "I'm sorry I didn't get your mom out. It never occurred to me that anyone would go after her, especially Beth."

Tessa points ahead of us to the other side of the street where the store is. "Me neither. But even if we did, Mom wouldn't have left that house. Rose Marie was like those people over there. Fear in action. She would have stayed put because Dad told her to just like those men over there are keeping their families trapped because someone told them to. All they have to do is rise up and they can overpower their keepers, but they're too afraid to charge the lawmen."

I tuck her hair behind her ear. "Maybe Chief gave a kill order so they're being smart, not fearful."

She looks over her shoulder. I shrug. "Don't give me those eyes, Tessa. Your buddy never had more than a marble, and now he's gone and lost even that. He *killed* the mayor and the mayor's wife. And then blamed us for it."

Her lips purse. "Chief is grieving, Warren. We all do stupid things when our hearts are broken and his was broken a long time ago. By your mother, who he never stopped loving for a single day of his life. That's why your mom hated me so much. She knew I was just like her and that I'd break you the way she broke Chief."

I drag a hand down my face. "Chief and my mom?"

Tessa leaves off trying to get a better view of what's happening across the street and fully turns from the water-soaked windshield, resting her hands on either side of my face. "They were together growing up, same as us, and then she dumped him, same as I dumped you. Then her life fell apart, same as mine, and now Chief is in the middle of all this blowback because he cared about me, same as you."

I slide a hand up her cheek and into her singed hair, the two of us piled in the van's passenger seat while Paul West and his people form a whisper puddle in the back. It isn't an ideal spot, but I'm learning to make time for the mushy stuff whenever I can. The way things keep changing, who knows if we'll have the chance for this again. "Tess, nothing about them is the same as us. I'd lock you up and never let you see daylight if you tried to drink yourself to death. That's why I finally put my foot down with Gary. I saw you going down all the wrong roads and no one around you was keeping you from it. I was willing to put up with a lot, but only if you were safe and living a good life."

She looks down at Bear's shirt. "You were living a good life. You had a business and Marcie. You might have loved me but you were going to marry Marcie, same as Chief married someone who wasn't your mom."

I rest my head on the back of the seat. "Some days I really wanted to marry Marcie. Those were the days when I truly hated you. But none of that ever stuck because I was just running through the motions of life until the day when I'd get to have an actual conversation with you. Until I had it out with you, for better or for worse, I couldn't let this go."

"I couldn't let it go either. I just..." She takes a deep breath and presses a hand back to the shoulder she hasn't complained about once. "I was only with Chopper because he couldn't hurt me. I cared about him something fierce, but it wasn't like it is with you. I could take him or leave him. Matt was..."

"A demon who walked through the gaping hole I left," I finish for her. "The worst is over, baby. We'll make it through tonight and then we'll get on to those new beginnings we were both so anxious for because that ring you found is yours. I bought it for you, not Marcie. The box is so dinged up because you've made me carry the dang thing around all of these years. It's time I put that diamond on your finger because I meant what I told Randy. I'm taking you home. That house I've been building has everything we ever talked about, even those fancy sheets from that hotel you liked."

Her eyes widen and I smile. It feels good to make her happy again. I brush my fingers over her beads. "I remembered everything, baby. Just wait until--"

"Grim." She whispers his name about a half second before I see the shadow in the side mirror. It's hard to make out anything beyond the inside of this vehicle but there's no mistaking Grim's ears. They're like funnel cakes stuck onto the side of his head, and those greasy ears are five feet behind the van.

I slide my hand to my gun. "Montrose did have an eye for the unsightly. Even Bear is a freak. No man should have limbs as thick as his."

Tessa slips her hand toward my second gun. "I don't know why you're choosing this moment to be judgmental, but where *is* Bear right now? I thought he was on the strays."

I smack her fingers and nod to the driver's seat. "I only know where you are and where you're going. Hop into that seat and use your one good arm to steer. We move on three."

She groans. "I can put the gun in my lap."

"No." I push her off me and toward the driver's seat. "Focus on steering, baby. Head straight for the lights in front of the store. I'll be right behind you."

"No," she growls, screeching my name when I move into the back of the van. "Warren, don't you dare get out of this van!"

The news people part for me like the Red Sea, fear pulsing out of them. I press a finger to my lips and ready myself to throw open the back door. My fingers touch the handle. Tessa hits the gas. I fly away from the door, shoulder slamming into the side of the van. I snap my head toward her. She grins in the rearview. "Nowhere but with me, *baby*."

I flip her off, a grin wider than the Grand Canyon splitting my stupid lips. I've missed the heck out of sniping with her.

Two shots ring out, wiping away both of our grins. The back of the van fishtails. From the sound of that pop, I'd say our back tires are gone. The vehicle skids and Tessa grounds out a painful curse, her one good arm struggling to right our course while the back of the van thumps across the pavement. She swerves hard to the left, slinging me overtop of the cameraman and sending the producer toppling into West. I push myself upright and head to the front, reaching her just as the van careens over the bank toward the Wiggly Pig parking lot.

I grab hold of the back of the driver's seat and push myself into place behind Tessa. "Taking a shortcut, sweetheart?"

Our front tires bounce into the already flooding lot, water splashing up around us. She lets go of the wheel, favoring her wounded arm. "Yeah, a shortcut straight into the creek that's looking a lot more like a river than the little stream we used to catch lizards in."

I spin the wheel, steering us away from the banks of the floodwater and straight into a collision course with the lights I told Tessa to drive to. "Hold on," I shout to the people in the back, swinging us hard to the left. The van teeters right, caught in a nasty mix of a hydroplane and a power slide. I work the pedals but I can't stop the vehicle's momentum. We're going to drill the concrete base of the massive light post. I throw my door open. "Out! Now!"

I haul Tessa out with me. We hit the parking lot, splashing into the two inches of water that's working its way to the front of the store. Metal crunches behind us. I cover Tessa's head, the van throwing itself into the concrete, the front end smashing to a dead stop while the back kicks up and twists midair, slamming roof-first into the pole. The trio of lights at the top groan, sending a shower of sparks raining onto the van. The three-headed lantern is coming down.

I let go of Tessa and race for the van. "West!"

"Here," his muffled voice answers. "We can't get out."

I check the driver's door. It's crunched and blocking half of the way out. The airbags are deployed and the front of the van is filled with debris. West's head is bobbing in the center of it all. I duck as more sparks shower down on us. "It's tight, but if you're not dead, there's room to get out. Move! Before that light brings a heap of electricity down into this water."

West shoves himself through the cramped space, blood trickling from the corner of his forehead. I shove my hands under his armpits and drag him away from the vehicle. A shot rings out, pinging off the underbelly of the van. I drop to the pavement, letting go of West and scrambling through the water like one of those lizards Tessa was talking about. The strays are good shots but between the curtain of rain and the wind, it's mighty hard to aim.

I reach the door of the van again, the smell of gasoline overwhelming. Now the strays don't have to be accurate enough to hit a person, these bullets they're slinging can blow us up. I stretch into the van and grab hold of the producer. "My leg," she groans.

I keep tugging. "If it's still attached, bring it with you."

The cameraman hoists her up from behind. The whole lower half of his face is a wreck, he's missing teeth and blood is dribbling through the holes. He huffs, pushing with all his might to get the uncooperative producer to move. I ho while he heaves and her torso breaks through the maze of airbags. I clear her from the van, her right leg bent at the calf, jutting out in an unnatural angle that looks like the break is as bad as the wailing currently ripping from her throat. The cameraman pushes out of the window behind her. "I've goth her," his voice hisses through the gaps in his teeth.

I nod. "Stay low and stay close." I spin away from them and keep my eyes on the other side of the road where we came from earlier. The strays are shooting but they haven't crossed into the lot. They know the Hinton charter is close and if they have to come and get us, they won't make it back out of this lot. That's why I told Tessa to get us under the lights. Expose us, and see if the strays will risk exposing themselves. I just didn't intend to get here quite like this.

I scurry to where Tessa is hunkered down with West behind a buggy return. The cameraman drags the producer behind us, doing his best to keep low despite the screaming coming from the woman. Between her, our crash, and the steady hail of bullets, we've drawn the attention of the cops inside the store. They're all at the front glass, guns in hand. I scrub the water out of my face. "Even if we didn't have a broken leg to deal with, we wouldn't make it around the building. The strays are expecting us to run for the others and they'll pick us off." I meet Tessa's eyes. "You have a way with pigs. Let's go sweet talk five of them."

~28~

Tessa

If it wasn't for the mother of all thunderstorms pouring down on us, that last bullet would have pierced Paul West's brain instead of pinging off a shopping cart. "Hurry." I urge West forward, he and his cameraman doing their best to drag their friend along in the wind and blinding rain. I fall in behind them. I need to keep these people moving because if Warren stops hearing our feet splashing through the water behind him, he's going to look for me. If he does that, he's going to lose the battle he's trying to have with the five lawmen whose guns are trained on him.

"Hibough!" I shout as the first set of automatic doors opens and Warren charges into the lobby, straight past the buggies and on toward the second set of doors where Hibough is positioned. Hibough glances my way, the barrel of his gun hesitating as it swings toward Warren. Not long enough for me to take another breath, but enough of a stammer for Warren to pull his trigger first. Two shots pop off, the bullets planting themselves in the soft spot where Hibough's vest doesn't protect what used to be his throwing arm.

Adding insult to the former quarterback's injury, Warren slams into Hibough, hooking under Hibough's vest and using the man as a shield as he barrels through the second set of automatic doors. I push past the cameraman, shoving buggies out of my way. There's no hesitation on Warren's part and I can already see who all the other cops are. These boys were on the football team. Warren never got along with a single one of them because the football team couldn't stand that Warren was faster than all their running backs, or that he had an arm better than anyone this side of the Mason-Dixon. Warren put them to shame while he was goofing off. He made fun of them and I was right beside him poking my own fun. The kids with school spirit took our lack of enthusiasm as a personal insult.

Warren uses Hibough's shoulder as a gun rest, aiming his weapon at the four pointing right back at him. "Take your best shot, piggies."

I dart around him and put myself between his gun and the others, holding my hands up. "We're not here to fight and we're not here alone, so don't shoot, because Warren patched into the club. Killing one wolf will make the rest of them trigger-happy. Not to mention that I'm a daughter of the Leidolf. All of you know that harming me is a death sentence. Gary being gone didn't change that. His death is only serving to make the others even more possessive than they were."

Sampson's jaw clenches, his head cocking to the left. "Hear those sirens echoing outside? We're not alone either. So move, Tessa, because your boyfriend just shot a cop."

Red and blue lights strobe hazily across the raincoated glass of the front windows. I take a step toward Sampson and point a finger at my bum shoulder. "My *fiancée* gave Hibough a little flesh wound to match the one Chief gave me. I fared better than Chief did in that encounter so if you don't want to end up like him, I suggest you put your gun down right now because to get to Warren, you go through me. You touch me, the club will have your head mounted above the door where Hibough's blood is currently splattered."

Eli steps backward, out of the line of four, his gun lowering. "Chief is dead?"

"Maybe," I answer, eyes narrowed on Sampson. "The same as you *may* be dead already, right along with those reinforcements you called for. You brought your men into a death trap. The club isn't who's out there shooting. We ran in here to get away from the snipers who are going to sit out there and pick off those reserves you think you have."

Sampson looks past me to where Hibough is groaning. "Let him go, because I put money on *our* snipers picking *you* off even with you being coward enough to hide behind another man."

I spin but Warren is faster. He brings the grip of his gun down on Hibough's head and shoves the wounded man toward the others, leaving himself open and vulnerable. "Tessa's been shot twice and hasn't cried about it once. You jocks turned pigs should take pointers from her because when the Leidolf get here, my brothers aren't going to be as nice or look as good."

I scramble to press my back against his front but as if he heard Warren's cue, Shaun launches one of his grenade cartridges. The explosion rattles the glass in the windows. Gasps and crying ring out of the center aisle of the store where kids are huddled with their parents, but it's the familiar sound roaring to life outside that has my own heart racing. The club is back on two wheels. Warren moves me aside and advances on Sampson, a grin cocking up one side of his mouth. "You always did choose the wrong uniform. The good guys are here though, and we're going to rescue these people you're trying to drown so you can either run along, or you can get on your knees and stay kneeling until the flood comes for you. I always heard pigs are good swimmers."

I shove myself into the inch of space between them, pushing back against Warren's chest. He slides a frustrated arm around my waist. "Don't worry, baby, these pigs don't know where their triggers are. If they did, they would have already used them."

Tim lowers his gun. "We're the law, we can't just go around shooting people. Especially in a room full of innocent people that we're trying to *save*, not drown."

Eli clears his throat. "Before you all barged in, we were making calls and trying to get a straight answer on what we're supposed to do about the flooding because people keep getting dropped off but no one gave us a way to get them out of here. Chief said--"

"I don't care what Chief said." I cut him off. "All of you were born with common sense and none of you used it. What would your sweet momma say if she knew you were holding these people hostage?" I look each man in the face. "What would your wives say? There are *children* here." I stop on Sampson. "The only cowards I know are ones who hide behind children."

Sampson shoves his gun into its holster. "We're not hiding and we're not hurting these people. None of us have used force on them and we're not pulling our triggers because we're not dumb enough to have a shootout in the middle of them!"

Drey holsters his gun, too. "Hibough tried to turn away the last cruiser full of people. He was told by that state trooper to shove his pipe where the sun don't shine."

Warren tsks. "And then I shot him. Just not your night, is it, Hibough?"

Hibough gives Warren a look that can scare the hair off a dog. But Warren's not a dog, he's a wolf, and he couldn't care less about Hibough or any of the others. "If you wouldn't have pointed your weapon at me *outside* of this room full of hostages, I wouldn't have given you those two love taps." He slides his hand into mine and pulls me to his side. "Keep your oinkers in check, Sampson, and those gunshots we're hearing outside these walls won't find their way in here."

Warren walks us toward townspeople we've known our whole lives. "You're all safe. The Leidolf are here to get you out of this place, whether that be out of Hinton or out of this store and back to your own houses. You're also welcome at Riverside Grille." He looks at me, water dripping off us and pooling on the avocado tile beneath our feet. "This is our town, and we're taking it the hell back."

~29~

Eli raids more of the medical supplies and hands bandages off to Valerie. She works at the pet clinic and is the closest thing to a doctor in the Wiggly Pig, a store never more aptly named. The cops locked in this supermarket with us are squirmy to say the least. There are motorcycles out front, not police cars. Shaun's grenade launcher is keeping the red and blue out of the parking lot. In return, the police aren't letting anything, including ambulances, through the line they're attempting to hold two miles around us, on the high ground.

The strays tucked tail when the club rode in, but none of the men with us know where Bear and his charter are so at any time the strays can attack us, the law, or both. They might be outnumbered but they already set a mountain on fire so I'm not putting any drastic measures past them. For all I know, they have a missile pointed at us.

I tug out another handful of baby wipes and mop up the blood on the floor next to where the producer's leg is freshly tied above the break. Her blood loss has slowed but she's still twisted up in pain even though Warren shared some of his pills with her. He's running low and this store doesn't have a pharmacy. We pulled over-the-counter drugs and I took some of those for myself, declining to dip into Warren's dwindling reserve. He's not even taking his anymore and the loss of his high is starting to show. As much as I prefer him sober, now isn't the time for it. He's pushing himself, and ever since Grim snuck up on us, he's stretched that push into a full-out shove.

"I've seen more blood lately than I ever cared to," I complain to no one in particular.

Eli drops down to help me wipe up the mess that we've all tracked through. "Half of the Wiggly Pig is covered in blood, thanks to you and Warren."

I stuff a gory wipe between Eli's service belt and his pants. "We're not the ones who decided to lock people up in a death trap."

He digs the bloody wipe out of his belt. "We believed in what our chief was telling us, that not letting anyone flee Hinton was the right thing to do. And even if we didn't, there was no choice given to us. This is the job we were ordered to do, and I think Momma will be more upset about those bikers blowing up the town than she's going to be about me doing my job."

I nod. "You're probably right. Be sure to tell her it was you and yours who blocked the ambulances. Especially if this lady here ends up dying. I bet your sweet momma will enjoy hearing how the cops brought people into a flood zone and then held off any chance they ever had of surviving."

Warren snorts, a sound I don't have to look to know who it's coming from. "The vans are on the way and the pigs will let us through or they'll be the ones dying tonight."

I rub my hands down the sides of Eli's arms, wiping blood on his uniform. "Well, there you have it straight from the wolf's mouth. No more innocent bloodshed in the Wiggly Pig tonight. All these people are going to get to go on living their lives. You and your reinforcements can call your momma and ask her for advice on how to get to hell the quickest."

Insulting Eli isn't helping matters but I can't stop myself. I should be out there hunting my sister right now, but instead, I'm stuck in this store making sure the town doesn't drown first. All because Chief and his merry band of idiots made these people sitting ducks. I get up off the floor and cross the aisle to Warren. He's freshly soaked from being ordered out into the raging darkness of the storm, his beautiful broken body being worked too hard, just to stave off a flood that's coming no matter what. "How bad is it out there?"

His throat works, shoulder pressed hard against the end of the shelving. "Flour bags aren't sandbags and there's only a handful of concrete barriers out there. The flatbed the club brought their bikes in on is about to float away. If it wasn't for the strays being in the wind again, we'd load people onto the back of it but it's too risky to have them out in the open."

I bite into the lip that I've chewed raw in the time I've been apart from him. I lower my voice. "And you? How bad are you hurting right now?"

He folds a hand over my hip and pulls me into him, his chestnut eyes scanning my face. "Same question, sweetheart, because we both look like we lost a fight with a grizzly."

I run my arms around him. "We're in this for better or for worse, right?"

He smooths the back of his fingers along my cheek. "What's between us is better than love and living apart from each other is worse than dying."

I rest my head against his chest and listen to the steady drum of his heart. "Good. Because I never forgot where I came from or who I belonged with. You're in my veins deeper than the mud of this town and no arms have ever felt better around me than yours."

Warren tucks a hand under my chin and brings my eyes to his, his lips twitching as a grin and a frown fight for dominance. "We were river rats together long before we were wolves. Us first, Leidolf second, and everything else any ol' place you'd like it." His lips fall against mine, our kiss deep and laced with the taste of the storm.

"Knock it off." Randy's gruff voice draws my tongue out of Warren's mouth. Randy thrusts his head toward the front of the store. "Go fetch the flatbed and load up any bikes that aren't being used, Gripr."

Warren stays where he is, his body putting most of its weight on the shelving unit and his hands holding me close to him. "I just got back inside, and I'm busy getting some lovin' from the pig charmer. Send Eli to do your fetching. I don't care for the way his mouth is drooling over what I'm doing with my woman."

"It's kind of hard not to watch," Eli defends, red-faced. "You're right out here in front of all of us."

Randy's fingers dig into my arm, words grinding between his teeth as he draws himself to my side. "Leidolf *first*."

Warren raises a brow at him. "So you and Eli both are spying on what I'm doing with *my* woman? Maybe I should start charging admission."

I push away from his chest. "Wolves are the only people my charm has ever worked on, Warren, and there was a time when I had a whole pack of them at my back instead of nipping at my heels." I meet Randy's glare. "I guess I didn't wholly erode your trust in me because you let me run with the plan that did exactly what I said it would. Beth came to me, like I knew she would, but I just happened to be shot and holed away in the back of a news van, so my sister just happened to escape again. Because that's what *nipping* gets you. Birds in bushes and nothing in hand."

I yank my arm free of his bruising grip and shove it around Warren. Not entirely because I want to show solidarity with him, but because he can use all the help he can get. "Come on, I'll help gather the bikes."

Randy falls in step beside me. "I have other plans for you, Tessa, because you *are* in my hand and the Gripr is going to let this happen. He's going to prove to me that he's a wolf."

I look up at Warren. This is a power move, just like the first time Randy sent Warren out into the rain, and I don't want Warren's defiance to give Randy cause to make our situation any worse. I tap his pill-holding pocket. "Go do what he wants, Warren. I'll be right here when you get back. Just don't get yourself shot out there."

Warren digs the satchel out, chewing only one of the few remaining pills, his eyes trained on Randy. "I don't have anything to prove to anyone. You know what I am. When we ride, Tessa comes with me."

He shoves out the door and into the rain. I stay beside Randy, letting him have the respect he needs from me right now because the night is long from over. "I want Beth."

Randy sighs. "You'll have her. She may not be in one piece but I've ordered her kept alive for you. And the Gripr will survive better if he keeps following my orders. You're doing right by telling him to."

I fold my arms over my chest. "We're falling in line and I'm doing my part to put power back into the hands of Leidolf. Hinton deserves to be restored to what it was. These kids deserve a better life than the one I've had, and I know the Leidolf can make that happen." I look at him. "So don't make the same mistakes Gary did. Don't focus on all the wrong things because Hinton can't afford you dropping the ball on them again. We *all* belong to you. Warren and I know that, and we're trusting that the club won't ever fail this town again."

I unclasp my arms and point to where West is doing exactly what I wanted him to. He's pillaging the prepaid phones and handing the best ones off to his cameraman. "These people know who locked them up and who is here to set them free. They'll sing the praises of the Leidolf and West will report it just the way we asked because he doesn't care if it's his own leg half hanging on, he's in this for the story that's going to make his career." I look at Randy. "He's documenting the club restoring order, getting the scoop of his lifetime and a way to account for each and every murder that has occurred in Hinton this summer without the club being attached to any. Except for Chopper killing my dad. Chopper is dead, though. And West's producer will be too if she doesn't get medical attention. So will all of these people if we don't get them out of here. We have to move them, and if the club has to kill all of those cops out there to do it, so much for power being restored to the Leidolf. West can't spin a massacre like that. So focus on *that* problem instead of worrying whether or not I'll put you before Warren because I won't, and he won't, and you're going to have to live with that or kill us both."

His eyes bore into mine. "I won't ever kill you, but I will kill him. Remember that the next time you decide to lecture me. I won't tolerate stray wolves." He yanks my hand forward and presses a cell phone into it. "Call Durand. I'm making him the new chief of police."

~30~

Sampson is skulking in the corner by the largest window along the front of the building. From here, he can see the lights of the law flashing in the sky beyond the knoll. "Do you want to save them?"

His eyes peel from their vigilant spot and rest on me. "I protect and serve, Tessa. So do they. All of those men and women out there aren't bad, they're just split and mixed up by infighting and outsiders trying to demand things be done their way."

His soft voice stirs its way into my gut, apprehension and fear thick in his delicate tone. "That's why the Leidolf are here. They're going to set this town right side up again."

Sampson shoves his hands into his pockets and glances to where West is conducting interviews with scared townspeople. "Was there ever a right side? Or are we all supposed to talk into that camera and say the Leidolf swooped in and saved the day, and now they're in charge because their law is the only law Hinton needs?"

I tap the phone against my palm. "If you want to go on record with the reporter, all you have to do is tell the truth. Let people know you followed bad orders because those were the only ones given by Chief Dunbar after he murdered the mayor in cold blood."

Sampson's eyes fly to mine. "Chief Dunbar didn't...he wouldn't..." Sampson looks away, the wheels turning in his head. "That son of a yellow-bellied snake. No wonder he spouted a bunch of orders right after the murder. None of them made sense but we followed them because he's always been good..." Sampson looks at me. "Chief was always a good man. I respected him."

I hold out the phone. "This summer is breaking the best of us, so help the Leidolf end it. Get Durand on the phone for me. He's going to be the new chief and his first order of business is to get those police cars out of the way."

Sampson tugs one of his hands free and scratches his neck. "Durand?"

I shove the phone into his chest. "The Leidolf *are* the law in Hinton, but the rest of you get to prance your pretty faces around pretending to keep that law. Durand has five minutes to clear the road. Anyone who follows him lives, anyone still in the road when the convoy comes, dies."

Sampson takes the phone and dials. "The five men in this store stood down for you, Tessa, and anyone out there who is loyal to Hinton's chief will do the same, but we're not all that's out there."

I look out to where Warren has pulled the flatbed right up in front of the window. "Trust me, I know exactly what's out there."

~

Sampson hands the elderly Mr. Green his cane and helps the man's curly-headed granddaughter into the back of the last van in line. Little Bella has lived with her grandpa since she was seven months old. The ladies in town used to go over and take turns helping the old man out and as Bella has grown up, she's become more of a child of this town than I ever was. Just about everyone has a claim to her. Until tonight, I'm sure that little eight-year-old has never been told no.

I let out a breath. It feels like all I've ever been told is no, people laying claim to me for their own purposes, not because I was ever special to them. My parents used me for whatever they could drain out of me, including the self-esteem they decided I shouldn't have. Chief looked out for me only because he wanted to steer me away from Warren. Beth twists and manipulates to get whatever her sick brain wants. And even Gary groomed me for the club, suggesting I become an accountant and offering up the office in the Grille. Looking back, I know Gary loved me something fierce. He wouldn't have stayed in touch with me all those years when he was gone if he didn't have love for me. But when he returned, I was as much of an opportunity as I was a daughter.

I wouldn't trade my years with Gary and I'd give anything to have it all back to the way it was, me working at the Grille with Gary and Chopper and every wolf I've loved. The only change I want in this life is Warren. I should have never left his side because Warren is the only person who hasn't used me for his own gain. All Warren has ever done is love me.

His sunbaked arms wrap around me from behind, corded muscles tightening around my waist. "That's the last of them, baby. Durand's police escort is waiting. Randy's taking everyone to the Grille, something West had a hand in. He hasn't finished getting his story so he's talked even the reluctant into staying with the club. He's going to make the Leidolf look like real heroes."

"They are," I answer. "*You* are. I'd be dead by now if not for you, and it's hard to say if I would have died by the hand of friend, foe, or family."

He moves his head over my shoulder, resting his cheek against mine. "It seems to me that you're still trying to get killed. How many times have I told you to stay inside, out of the storm, and away from the windows?"

I lift a hand to his soaked hair. "No one is going to shoot me. Besides, you're out here and I go where you go. Remember?"

He turns his lips to my cheek, plants a kiss and then bites my ear. "You mean again? Because people already shot you, so stop trying to sweet-talk me. Go get your fine behind in the flatbed. We're going to haul these bikes back to Riverside and then I'm going to eat my last three pills and rip out your sister's throat."

"Romantic." I grin, sliding my hand down into his and catching Sampson's eye. He nods. I nod back, giving the truce we all want. Sampson closes the van door and Zeno's bike roars into place behind it, Shaun beside him, a massive gun strung over Shaun's shoulder. The men don't talk a lot about themselves but a tattoo on Shaun's arm names him as ex-military. Not an uncommon thing to see in the three-patch world. I just didn't know he was trained in explosives because to my knowledge, the club has never had to use the force they've used this summer.

Warren opens the driver's side door of the flatbed and I climb onto the seat. "Want me to drive, Gripr?"

He pulls himself up beside me. "I want you to sit as close as you can and paw me like you used to do in our van."

I laugh, relief washing through me. "You make me happy, Warren. Even in a time when there shouldn't be an ounce of happiness to be had."

He starts the engine and gets in line behind Zeno and Shaun. "Just grope me, baby, because you really suck at sweet-talking. And at following orders. And cooking." He turns my way with a wink. "But you're really good at repeating my own words, and extra good at being the most exciting thing I've ever seen."

I relax against his shoulder, letting my hand sit higher on his thigh than it should. The flatbed's tires splash through the floodwater that will soon be too high for the remaining motorcycles. "Are we going to make it back to the Grille without having to rescue those bikes?"

Warren follows the convoy. "I'm bringing up the rear for that very reason, baby. If they need us, we'll be here to save their sorry butts."

Durand's convoy pulls out on the road ahead of ours, making a train of vehicles splashing through the flooded streets. Cars are abandoned on the roadsides and the houses we pass are dark, as if all of Hinton has abandoned their post. Outside of the lights flashing ahead of us, the only other lights are coming from the east. "Is that an ambulance?"

Warren stiffens, slowing at the intersection. "Looks like, and it's in a hurry."

Zeno goes on through the intersection with the others but Shaun stops because the flatbed can't make it through without holding up the ambulance. I shift in my seat. "What's that behind them?"

Warren lays on his horn. "Bear." He revs forward, trying to get Shaun to move. Instead, Shaun gets off his bike and readies his gun. Warren spews out curses, pulls his gun, and pushes my head down. "If Bear is chasing that ambulance, strays are inside of it."

My face hits the seat but I don't need to see to know what I'm hearing. Shaun just fired, the boom ringing out ahead of screeching tires and crunching metal. I can almost feel the fire of the explosion on my skin, but it's the cool metal of the barrel pressed to my temple that I'm focused on. So much for Warren and me making light of our situation. Grim and his big ears are leaning over the back of the bench seat, ruining our fun. Those wings on the side of his head are practically flapping as he smiles at Warren. "Make a left, Gripr. A special lady wants to see you, and she says I can have her sister. Dead or alive. I'd prefer to have Tessa alive, so she can *suck* at more than sweet-talking."

~31~

Warren

I slide my pistol onto the dashboard, lifting my foot from the brake and letting the flatbed drift forward. Shaun looks up at me, his assault rifle fitted with a UBGL that just took out the ambulance. He's not the only one with those kinds of toys, though. The strays were once wolves and they set this trap as if they still are.

"Grim, I'm real tired of people thinking they can touch what's mine." I hit the gas. Shaun rolls forward, body splashing into a ditch no longer capable of containing the water it was meant to hold. He comes up out of the muck in a rain of bullets, launching another fiery round toward the burning ambulance where Antonio is lighting up Bear and Evan, keeping the northerners pinned down in a ditch of their own.

I swing my wheel to the left, just like Grim wanted, the roar of bikes heading back our way overpowering the assault his partner is rolling out. Like the smart girl I know her to be, Tessa uses the momentum of my hard turn, letting it slide her head out from under Grim's barrel. I let go of the wheel and send an elbow into his face. His head slams into the glass behind him, his gun discharging and putting a bullet through my windshield. "Run!" I shout to Tessa, pain bursting through my twisting torso as I launch over the back of the seat. Grim swings, his fist finding purchase in my already busted ribs. The tip of his gun shoves up underneath me and I throw myself sideways, unlodging the gun before he can shoot. I bring his head with me, slamming it into the side of the cab. His gun slips and I jam my elbow into his neck. He brings his forearm up, cutting across my face. Blood bursts in my mouth and I spit it into his eyes, hooking a punch into his jaw. He returns the favor, fists and spit spraying until I don't know which one of us it's coming from. Tessa lunges over the seat, hammering her fist down on Grim's head. "Dammit, woman," I growl. "I said for you to go!"

She switches from hammer fist to elbow. "Not without you!"

I push off of Grim, throwing myself backward, an arm shoved into Tessa's middle and the other hand drawing my spare gun. Grim heaves over the top of the seat. I bury my gun in his big ear and pull the trigger.

Tessa's arms swarm around me, her hands moving to the ribs she knows aren't healing like they should. I wrap my hand around her arm and shove the door open, pushing her out into the rain and keeping hold of her while I get my feet under me. "Another thing I'm real tired of is you not listening to me." I shove her forward, away from the bullets and down beside the flatbed's big tires. "I don't tell you to run because I want to be a damn martyr. I tell you to run so I can kill the sons of Satan without you having to see it!"

She squirms to get free of my grip. "It's a little late for that, don't you think?"

I get on my knees beside her, my breath shallowing to a wheeze. "What I think, is that this is life and death and I intend for both of us to live."

I dig out the last of my pills, sucking in a swell of air and biting into my tongue as pain radiates through me. She slaps at the water lapping over our legs. "At least we're in our element. We can't get to the river so it's coming to us."

"The river's not the only thing coming," I nod to where Zeno is stomping toward us, the flames of the ambulance crash behind him painting him like a demon walking straight out of hell. "Looks like the cavalry is finally showing up for us."

I toss back the last of my precious pills and open my mouth to the rain. It washes everything down my throat. Drugs, blood, and Tessa. I wipe the water from my face and glare at Zeno. "By my count, there's a heck of a lot more of us than there are of those strays, so tell me exactly why I was just made to kill another one in front of my woman? Who in the hell you came from let Grim get in my flatbed?"

Zeno's chest heaves. "I think we still have a traitor among us. When I find them, they die."

Tessa's head swivels toward him. "The strays are working with Beth. Grim wanted to take us to her."

He reaches a hand down to her, teeth scraping as his anger fights against the control he's trying to keep. "Get off the ground and come with me."

She shuffles to my side. "No, thanks. I'll stay with Warren until you figure out who is letting our enemies group themselves together to rise against us."

His boots splash forward and he squats down, the flicker of that fire working overtime on the pissed-off wolf. "You're going to the Grille, and you're going to stay there until we gut your sister and every last person who ever thought they could stand against the Leidolf." His eyes cut to mine. "They *all* die."

~

Beth

"Antonio is boxed in and I assume Grim is dead since the Gripr and your sister are still with the Hinton Charter," Cedar reports, lowering binoculars that are nicer than the ones I've used in the past. The ones I lost because I was forced to run out of the Bridgewater house with nothing but the clothes on my back.

I fold my arms beneath my chest, plumping up the boobs none of these stupid men are even looking at. I tried to screw Grim and Cedar both, but neither of them looked at me like I was anything special. I didn't even get any favors from Hank when he came with the spare keys for the flatbed. I puffed up his ego, told him how smart he was while undoing his pants, and all he did was shove me aside. He wanted Millie, the little Baker tramp that the rest of them have been getting off on. I could hear her crying the instant Antonio shoved me into the doublewide the hussy and her parents live in. She acted like she didn't enjoy being tied to that bed but I could see in her eyes how exciting it all was for her. Five men ravaging her, their desire for her sprayed all over her body, mixing with the trickles of blood and those fake tears she cried for them. When I took the scissors to her, her tears were real.

I look at Cedar. He's built like Warren, long and lean, wrapped in the kind of muscle that doesn't tire out like the bulk Matt carried. Like what's covering Bang who's on the other side of me, squishing me in the middle of our pickup's bench seat. These gang members with their nicknames think they get to call the shots instead of listening to me. "You smell like wood, Cedar, so I get the name, but why do all of you use street names? The Hinton Charter doesn't. Except for that moron Chopper."

Cedar looks down his nose at me. "How do you know their names are real?"

I fidget with my shirt, pulling the neck down just in case more cleavage will finally get Cedar to come to his senses. I never considered that gang members would choose normal names as their fake ones, but I don't recall ever hearing last names to go with any of them outside of Gary. I don't think any of the women in town who *married* those bikers even changed their last names. My face heats. "They're all liars. Every single one of them. When do we kill them? I want them all dead."

"Wait for it," Bang murmurs, opening his passenger door and swinging his hulking frame up into the back of the pickup. He taps the glass and Cedar puts the rig he stole from Bobby Baker into gear. That stupid wannabe fireman shouldn't have been trying for his five minutes of fame if he wanted to keep his wheels.

The charges Bang set go off, a fiery flare of smoke showing us right where the road opened up, creating a chasm the rest of the Leidolf can't cross. They can double back, but they can't help Tessa. She's cut off from her lap dogs and unless she wants to drown, she can only run in one direction. I hope she does. It'll be fun to chase her down the road. A smile creeps over my lips. "Can I drive?"

Cedar glances at me, his eyes finally dropping to my chest. "You're a sick little nymph. Take the wheel and aim for the wolf with the biggest gun. Bang and I will do the rest."

When these shaggy northerners picked me up outside Tessa's neighborhood, I thought they were going to kill me. Instead, they ran with me. They think they can use me. I slide under Cedar, excitement pulsing through my center as his body pushes across mine. He moves like Warren. Fluid and strong. Confident. I want him. I want Warren. And I want my sister to watch. I flip on Bobby's emergency lights and press my foot against the gas pedal. "They're mine, Tessa. They're all mine."

~32~

Tessa

Sirens and gunfire, two things I've heard enough of. The sounds fill the air and Warren shields me as another blast tears up the asphalt around us. "They're blocking us in," I scream through the noise.

"I can see that," he answers, hands splashing in the water around us as he moves me toward the front of the flatbed where Zeno is tucked against the hood returning fire. "We need to get across the intersection. When I say move, you run like you've never run before. The water on that side isn't as deep but it's still enough to slow you down. Don't let it, Tess. You run and you keep going until you find Randy and the others."

I look behind us. The floodwaters have breached the Wiggly Pig by now and with the way what's in the streets behind us is rising, before long, not even the flatbed will be safe. Nothing on this side of the road is going to survive the flood. "You're coming with me, Warren."

He plasters a palm against my cheek. "Always, baby. You run and I'll be right there chasing you."

I close my eyes to the flashes of old memories. The ones where I was running for fun, Warren's smiling face and deep laugh filling me full. Him catching me was sweeter than honey. Warmer than the brightest July day. I don't know where our childhood went but I wish we could have it all back.

"Move!" he shouts, pushing me forward.

I sprint into the fray, the blast of Shaun's gun shattering my eardrum. I stumble. Warren catches my shirt and pushes. "Go, go, go!"

Lights flash to my right, barreling toward the intersection the same way the ambulance did. Shaun steps into the road in front of it. Bear and Evan advance through the muddy water, covering Shaun as he reloads. Cedar hangs out the window of Bobby Baker's truck, lighting up his former brothers. I focus back on the space in front of me and pump my legs. Warren's gun cycles through all its bullets, aiming at the shell of the ambulance Antonio is rounding. Warren shoves me to the ground. My face slams into the soupy gravel, water sucking into my lungs mid-breath. I swing my head up, coughing and sputtering. Warren is gone.

I spin around, scrambling over the ground. Warren is running toward Antonio. The man is slumped over the twisted metal of the wrecked ambulance, his head now only a chin. I scream but Warren keeps going, tossing his empty pistol and ripping the rifle out of the dead man's hands. I race after him. He jumps over a downed tree and clears a hole made by one of Shaun's grenades. A cackle shrieks through the night. My blood runs cold. Beth is here.

I leave off my pursuit of Warren and round the front of the smoking ambulance, searching the fog for the hyena. The sound she's crowing makes it easy. I meet her cold stare with one of my own. She's behind the wheel of Bobby's truck. Her eyes rip from mine and I follow her trajectory. "No!" I scream, but Beth isn't slowing down and Shaun isn't moving. He's fiddling with his jammed gun. I run for him but I'm too late. Beth plows through him, leaving part of his scalp clinging to the bumper of Bobby's truck.

She swerves and comes right for me. I return the favor, running as hard as I can toward that truck. There's shouting, and bullets are piercing the metal of her rig, but Beth keeps coming and I keep going.

A shadow cuts into my vision, airborne as the pickup gets closer. Beth swerves again, missing me, and cackling as I get a good view of what's toppling over her tailgate. "Warren!" I scream. His head flips up, eyes locking on mine. I run after him, arms and legs burning, tears rushing down my face. "Jump!" I shout. A dark form rises out of the truck bed behind him. Bang's big fist drops onto Warren's head, sending the newly acquired rifle flopping out of the truck. "No!" I scream, heart ripping out of my chest as I watch his body go limp. I run harder. Screaming. My pleas answered only by the rapidly fading taillights.

The ground around me vibrates. "Tessa!" Zeno calls my name. I don't answer. I just keep running, the rain washing down my face as fast as the tears. An arm slings around me. Zeno hoists me from the earth and plants me in front of him, Shaun's bike underneath us. Bear and Evan race past us. "Follow them!" I scream with everything I have left. "Follow them!"

Zeno picks up speed, gaining on the bikes ahead of us. Lights and sirens erupt from my left. A police SUV careens out of the field and onto the road. Durand is driving and Randy is riding shotgun, window down and gun ready. Zeno falls in behind them. "The tunnels," I shout. "Beth is heading for the tunnels!" In every fiber of my being, I know where she's heading, because she can't outrun the club now but she'll still try for one last kill and she'll want to drop Warren's body in a place where his death holds meaning for me. Another place she can defile what Warren and I consider special. *Ours*. It isn't enough for her to hurt me, she wants her taint to cover every happy memory I've ever had.

"Stop here," I order Zeno, placing my hands over his. He pulls to the side of the road. Everyone else keeps going, chasing Bobby's truck and avoiding the bullets being sprayed by the two remaining strays.

Zeno rests his hands on his thighs. "Your sister dies tonight. If you don't want to see it, I'll take you to the Grille where you're supposed to be."

I get off his bike. "Bobby's truck can't outrun our motorcycles. Beth knows that. She plans to make it to the park where she murdered Granger and Gary. She wants to get into the tunnels."

I head off down the hill, not far from where I jumped over the cliff when Freddie was chasing me off the mountain. "I can get in the tunnels behind her. You don't have to come but I need your gun."

Zeno follows me, grabbing my elbow when I start to slide in the mud. "I trust you know where your sister is going. Get us into the tunnel and I'll let you have your choice of my weapons."

I pick my way down the dark and slick hillside, Zeno's steady grip never leaving me. The rain lets up and I take that as a sign. Beth's life is meant to end tonight and whoever is watching from above is making my path to her a little bit easier. When I reach her, they better hope they've also seen fit to keep Warren alive.

I lead Zeno down to the fencing that separates the old tunnel from the new. Beth will have no choice but to run for the old one, it's the easiest entrance. "This way." I skulk along the fencing, toward the echo of dripping water, thankful for all the years I played hide-n-seek in the woods with Warren. Beth always wanted to play with us and now she'll get her chance. I'll hide in the shadows of the tunnel and seek a bullet right through her cold heart.

Low and silent, I move through the night like I'm part of it, Zeno and me slipping quietly through the branches jutting out around the back edge of the tunnel. I arch our path out to the right, setting a course to weave around the discarded pile of railroad ties that are rotting up ahead. I doubt Beth will figure anyone can navigate this mildewed hall without light and I guarantee that she can't. She'll need to illuminate her surroundings because it's one thing to turn off your light so you can sneak a hundred feet into a cave with no obstacles to speak of, but she wasn't a voyeur when I was alone in this tunnel with Warren. She might have heard us in here, but she didn't sneak into this crumbling den of traps without us catching her.

Fifty yards in, I cut back across the forgotten tracks. Zeno keeps his hand on me and follows me step for step, like sound is not a thing he's capable of producing. Beth is though. I can hear her over the eruption of gunfire echoing back to us. I turn to Zeno, whispering amid the concealing noise. "Let Randy know we're in here."

Zeno takes his hand from me and straining the patience Warren doesn't think I have any of, I lower down into a crouch while Zeno sends Randy the message. We conceal the light from his phone, preferring to take the chance on it being seen than on getting blown up by the Leidolf who have arrived on the other side.

Zeno shows me his screen. Randy sent back a picture of Cedar's head lopped down the side of Bobby's truck, blood dripping from it and the side mirror. I swallow. "And Warren?"

"Not in the truck." Zeno shows me the second picture. Hank sprawled on the ground, blood bubbling from his still warm body. "We found our traitor. Only Bang is left, and he's just inside the entrance to this tunnel, trying to pick off our boys."

I reach for Zeno's gun, replaying the faces of the dead. My mind hangs on Gary's gentle smile and the sound of Chopper's rare chuckle, the reel ending with my mom's hollow eyes. Hers was a life stunted, one without a single dream championed or a solitary wish granted. She was born to sorrow and married to shame. Her only hope of escape was the life she could have lived after Chopper rid her of the shackles she was too hopeless to remove herself. Beth stole that fresh start from our mother. Now I'm going to steal the soul from my sister's body.

Zeno puts his phone away and lowers to my ear. "Beth is yours, Bang is mine."

I grip the gun at my side. "Deal."

~33~

We move silently through the tunnel, closing in on our prey. An occasional shot echoes back to us but Randy's not attacking. He's letting Bang waste ammo.

I focus on the sounds. The drips and the noises drifting to us, the way they're bouncing off the old walls to make the inside of this tunnel sound more like a concert than a dark hole through a mountain. I used to play this game with Warren. Sit in the darkness and listen to sounds distorting themselves through the tunnel. Sometimes we'd hear voices, people walking into the front of the tunnel where there was still light enough to see. Sometimes we'd throw rocks and growl when select few would bring flashlights and attempt to make it through to the other side. We were kids goofing off, trying to claim any spot we could for ourselves, without any understanding that what we were doing then would mean so much to us now.

Beth has a light on the ground next to her, a cell phone shining up to the top of the tunnel while she kneels at Warren's back, fiddling with what looks to be handcuffs. She probably lifted those from the police car she stole. I scan Warren's face. He doesn't look dead, just slumped against the wall unconscious. Bear is the only person I've ever seen who's bigger than Bang and apparently Bang is aptly named.

Warren's head lolls to the side, a moan slipping out of his mouth. Beth moves her hands from the metal cuffs clasping his wrists together, running her fingers through his hair and putting her lips against his ear. "That's it, baby. Wake up and let me see those eyes."

She runs her tongue over the curve of his ear and my stomach rolls. I slink from the darkness, gun outstretched. "Beth, get away from him."

She startles, her body cramming behind Warren's as tightly as she can get it. She pulls a knife from the ground beside her and holds it to his throat, her free hand fisting in his hair and pulling his head back to give her more room. "You're early, but I can still work with this."

She tucks the knife tight against his throat and presses it into his skin. Blood trickles from underneath the blade. "Don't!" I shout.

She laughs. "Oh, but you're going to love this, Tessa. Just watch." Her mouth moves back to Warren's ear, her big tongue jutting out and flattening against Warren's lobe, rolling over his skin as she purrs. "Mmm, see how much he likes it. Me, Tessa. He likes *me*."

Warren's eyes blink open, glassy and dazed. He looks at me, scanning the gun pointed at him. "You have a gun on me, Tessa."

I nod. "Beth has her tongue in your ear."

The sensation registers, his surroundings coming into focus. He gasps, slamming his head backward. Beth ducks out of the way and digs her knife deeper into the neck I used to kiss as we lay under the stars. "Stop!" I scream, his blood painting that beautiful tan of his red, running down his neck and over his collarbone. He tries to get up but it only deepens the cut. "Don't move, Warren," I beg. "I'm going to need you to hold real still for me."

Beth cackles, the sound of Bang's footfall growing ever closer. "You should see the look on your face right now, baby sister. It's almost better than when you found Gary." She makes a face. "What are you going to do? Shoot yourself before Bang gets here? Or let him pin you underneath him so Warren can watch you doing what you do best while you watch me cut the heart right out of his chest?

I walk toward her, Bang's shadow coming into focus. "Warren?"

He swallows, the motion forcing more blood from his neck. "Yeah, baby?"

I stare into his eyes. "Do you trust me?"

He stills, so completely he isn't even breathing. His lips part. "I trust you with my life. And Beth's as wide as a barn so you do what you have to do, baby. I love you in this life and all the ones to come."

A tear drips from my lashes. "I love you, Warren. And I go where you go, in this life and all the ones to come."

I pull the trigger.

~

Morning is almost here. I sit on the bumper of an ambulance watching the news on the phone Zeno left me. His aim on Bang was perfect, the blade sticking out of the throat of the last stray standing evidence of that. But Zeno alone isn't the one the news is hailing as a hero. Paul West is at

Riverside Grille, telling the world that the Leidolf were instrumental in bringing closure to a town ripped apart by murder and betrayal.

I watch the footage, the Grille full of people, not all of them rescues from the Wiggly Pig. Townsfolk have gathered to be with their loved ones. Or came because they're still scared and would rather be surrounded by the Leidolf than in their own homes. Durand is even encouraging them to gather with the club. He left the tunnel shortly after all the threats to Hinton were put down and has been on location outside the Grille ever since, being interviewed by Paul West and assuring the people of Hinton that our town is now safe.

I look away from the screen as he speaks of Chief Dunbar, sorrow thick in his voice. "The stress of duty was too much for our former chief, driving him to act alone in murdering the mayor, the mayor's wife, and attempting to corrupt the rest of the force before taking his own life tonight."

I guess Dunbar can't tell all of Hinton that Chief died when my house blew up, but Chief meeting his end by his own hand isn't fitting for the lawman. "Make no mistake," Durand's voice crawls out of the phone. "With our sorrow fresh in our hearts and our loved ones held close, Hinton will rise again."

Warren climbs from the interior of the ambulance, sitting on the bumper next to me. He lifts the phone from my lap. "You did this, Tess, you brought the town back together."

I meet his eyes, heart aching with the pain of everything we've lost. The bandage across Warren's neck and the scars on his face reminders of the evil this world holds.

Warren slouches against me, his warm hand cupping my face. "I can hear your thoughts, woman. Don't you dare get sad on me again because we're not fighting today. We're celebrating. And we're not stopping until long after you walk down the aisle to me because for once in your life, you hit what you were aiming for."

He's right. My bullet skirted over his shoulder the way I intended, keeping its course straight through Beth's eye and out the back of her head. Once Warren was out of the way I shot her again. Through the other eye. The matching wounds seemed fitting for her.

I wrap my arms around him. The footage of the inside of the Grille made my stomach flip and my head race with memories. "When Gary first returned to Hinton, I asked if he'd walk me down the aisle. Do you remember?"

Warren brushes his fingers under my eye. "I was there, baby. He said he'd give me your hand and that you could give me your heart, but that his Tessa would always belong to the Leidolf."

I nod, whispering to him so the nearby wolves won't hear. "The club will give us today, maybe even tonight, but then Randy's going to use me to test you. Pass that test, Warren. Prove your loyalty to the club. Show them there's nothing left in us to break, and then maybe Randy will allow us to plan the wedding I owe you."

Warren straightens, keeping an arm fixed firmly around me. "Randy doesn't have a say in this. I'll follow his lead and fall in line when it has to do with the club, but we've both answered for everything we're going to. Not a man in this world holds the power to keep us apart." He tucks a hand under my chin. "These paramedics hooked me up with some morphine. I can get us to our van. And you deserve a vacation after what you just did for this whole dang town, so get your pretty little self up and tell me where you want to go for our honeymoon."

Hinton was fine before Beth and Montrose decided to tear this town apart, and I can't take any credit for helping to put it back together. Not after so many of my actions stoked the flames that brought us to this place. But with Gary gone and every trace of Chopper having already been wiped clean, nothing in this place feels like it's mine anymore. Nothing except for Warren. I run my hand the length of his arm, stopping just beneath where the worst of his burns are. "Maybe we should take Bear up on his offer and go north for a while? I hear it's so flat up there you can watch your dog run away for two miles straight."

A grin flits over Warren's face. He stands, bringing me up with him. "Mrs. Gripr, is that your way of telling me you want a puppy?"

I tighten my hand in his, moving with him toward the roar of the overfilled river below the tunnels. Dawn is breaking through clouds that are finally leaving Hinton. "A puppy. And a few babies." I glance to where Randy is leaning on the side of Bobby's pickup truck. "And no more fighting. When Randy says we can't keep walking down this hill, please just listen. We can make do with what we're given."

Warren bends, swinging me up into his arms. A show of strength that he shouldn't be giving. His lips brush mine. "Yes to the dog, and we'll get started on those babies just as soon as we reach our van." He turns back to the truck, eyeing Randy. "We'll be at home. Don't bother us. I'll let you know when we're ready to check in again."

"Tessa." My name spills from lips that aren't Randy's. Every muscle in Warren's body tenses. He turns slowly toward the brush below the tunnel, the spot from which a voice we never thought we'd hear again is calling my name. Chief is standing at the edge of the shadows, wild-eyed, and his clothes as bloody and wrecked as his face. Warren lets out a growl.

"Tessa." Chief's focus stays on me, his gun at his side. "You were right. You're to blame for all of this. It's your fault they're all dead."

Warren sets me on my feet. "That's not the way I see it and in a second, you're not going to be seeing anything at all."

Chief's glassy eyes blink and he raises his gun. "Say your last words, honey, and I'll make your end quick. Same as they'll make my death quick."

I look around us. Rick is standing with Randy, their guns trained on Chief. Zeno is off to our right, knives in his hands. I slide my palm onto the crook of Warren's elbow and pull him away from Chief, my lips giving those last words to a man who's been a part of my life for as long as Warren has. "Chief, you only ever had two ways out of this mess. Eat your own gun or seek vengeance. Those are the same choices I've been faced with. We both chose right. Vengeance." I slide my hand down Warren's arm and curl my fingers through his, a tear tracking down my face as I stand shoulder to shoulder with the man I more than love while another I care about loses his life.

The club hits their mark. Chief drops to the ground before he ever fires a shot. I look up at Warren, visions of a long-ago summer day dancing through my mind. We stood on a cliff like the one behind the Grille, Samantha swirling around, her arms spread wide and her hair shining in the sunlight. Life was full back then. Happy. We were free, and wild with the beat of a future we were sure was ours for the taking. Now, we'll never be free. Too much blood has been spilled, and Warren will be forced to fight for any scrap of a future we're allowed to have. I tighten my hand in his. "I don't want this. I want those wings Samantha promised we'd have one day."

A smile splits his lips, spreading up through his chestnut eyes and down to where his hand crushes mine. "Then let's fly, baby."

My steps match his. We turn our backs on the club, our strides long and powerful. Randy shouts.

Rick.

Zeno.

The voices of the living and the dead rising up all around us.

I smile as big as Warren is. We were rats long before we were wolves, and the sweet taste of freedom is waiting for us at the end of a roaring current. Our feet crash into the raging waters, bodies tucked tightly together as the heavy flow of the flood drags us. Warren throws his head back, a howl breaking from his chest. I let my own rip loose, our message echoing over the face of the water for all of Hinton to hear. We belong to each other, and the world belongs to us.

This is how it was always meant to be. Warren, me, and our fate decided by the river that raised us.

Acknowledgments

"Great is the art of beginning, but greater is the art of ending." ~ **Lazurus Long**

When I started this trilogy, I had no idea where it would lead. I had one good ending to the first book and little else. I let the characters guide me, telling their stories the way they wanted them told even when it ripped out my own heart. I love them all. I appreciate the way each character revealed themselves to me and I will carry them with me always. One day, maybe I'll revisit Hinton.

To the readers and die-hard fans of this series – THANK YOU! Every time a book is read, another character is born. It's through your feedback that I'm able to hone my craft, delivering what you like about my writing style, and the twisty plots you tell me you love the most. Words can never express the depths of my gratitude.

RISE

Rise wouldn't have been finished without the support of my husband, son, daughter-in-law, and loads of puppy cuddles. There were even a few kitty scratches obtained during the writing of this manuscript. But mostly, my patient editor kept me from jumping off the cliff. Anita's wisdom is priceless.

About the Author

Lee Dawna is a thriller and suspense author, and host of the Immortal Monsters Podcast. An avid traveler and outdoorswoman, you may bump into her along a remote trail where a meandering stream whispers her next story.

Visit **LeeDawnaBooks.com** for more on what the author is up to lately, and to **join her mailing list** for special announcements.

ALSO BY LEE DAWNA

<u>Beller Ties – A four-book stand-alone romantic suspense collection.</u>

Something So Beautiful

Now And Always

Dawn Of Devotion

Marked By Forever

<u>Hinton Thriller Series – A serial-killer thriller trilogy.</u>

Descend

Smother

Rise

Coming September 1, 2023 – *Sierra*, a modern stand-alone thriller. Join the mailing list for early release news!